"It Was My Kiss, Wasn't It?"

"What?"

"I kissed you last night. You kissed me back. We've been too intimate. You swore you'd never kiss another man, and you did. Now you're running off to Atlanta to hide."

"How can you joke?" Bridget sputtered.

"Because high melodrama isn't my style, and I hope to heaven it isn't yours. Not when there's so much at stake."

"Matthew Branigan, for all I know, my sisters instructed you to kiss me."

"I thought of that kiss all by myself. After the demands of medical school, it was a relief to know that I remembered how."

"You *are* turning this into a joke."

"It was worth a try. I didn't get very far being serious. I only kissed you because you'll need a point of reference—Yankees as compared to Southerners. I never would have considered it if I thought you might change your mind and stay up here."

"Well, you should have made that clear. My response was hardly my best effort."

Dear Reader:

Sensual, compelling, emotional . . . these words all describe Silhouette Desire. If this is your first Desire, let me extend an invitation for you to sit back, kick off your shoes and enjoy. If you are a regular reader, you already know what awaits you—a wonderful love story!

A Silhouette Desire can encompass many varying moods and tones. The books can be deeply moving and dramatic, or charming and lighthearted. But no matter what, each and every one is a terrific romance written by and for today's women.

I know you'll love March's *Man of the Month*, *Rule Breaker* by Barbara Boswell. I'm very pleased and excited that Barbara is making her Silhouette Books debut with this sexy, tantalizing romance.

Naturally, I think *all* the March books are outstanding. So give into Desire . . . you'll be glad that you did!

All the best,

Lucia Macro
Senior Editor

LESLIE DAVIS GUCCIONE
PRIVATE PRACTICE

SILHOUETTE *Desire*

Published by Silhouette Books New York

America's Publisher of Contemporary Romance

For Kevin, Drew, Sean, Ryan, Jody and Matt,
who gave me the best time a writer can have on paper

and my editor, Isabel Swift,
who encouraged me to bring all the Branigans to life
It's been wonderful!

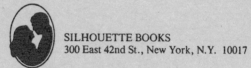

SILHOUETTE BOOKS
300 East 42nd St., New York, N.Y. 10017

ISBN: 0-373-05554-4

First Silhouette Books printing March 1990

Printed in the U.S.A.

LESLIE DAVIS GUCCIONE

lives with her husand and three children in a state of semichaos in a historic sea captains' district south of Boston. When she's not at her typewriter she's actively researching everything from sailboats to cranberry bogs. What free time she has is spent sailing and restoring her circa 1827 Cape Cod cottage. Her ideas for her books are based on the world around her. As she states, "Romance is right under your nose." She has also written under the name Leslie Davis.

BRANIGAN FAMILY TREE

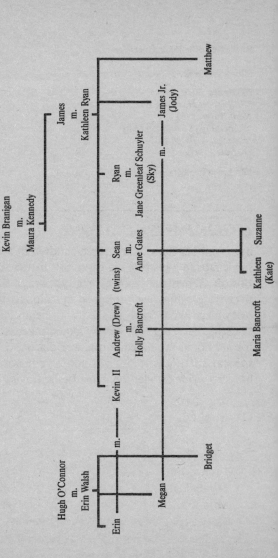

Hugh O'Connor
m.
Erin Walsh

Kevin Branigan
m.
Maura Kennedy

Erin — Kevin II — m. — Kevin II — Andrew (Drew) — Sean — Ryan — James — Matthew
Megan   (twins)   m.   m.   m.
Bridget   Holly   Anne   Jane   Kathleen Ryan
                        Bancroft   Gates   Greenleaf
                                               Schuyler
                                               (Sky)

James Jr.
(Jody)

Maria Bancroft   Kathleen   Suzanne
                        (Kate)

One

Bridget O'Connor sighed and scanned the dog-eared newspaper clipping, which she had nearly committed to memory.

The Millbrook Ledger,
Millbrook, Massachusetts, March 3

AROUND TOWN

Hugh S. O'Connor of Valley View Farm, Dean's Corner, New Jersey, announces the engagement of his daughter Erin Flynn to Kevin Patrick Branigan II, both of Millbrook. She is also daughter of the late Erin Flynn O'Connor.

Miss O'Connor is a graduate of the Warren County, New Jersey, schools and Centenary College. She received her master's degree in Public

Health from Drew University and is currently director of women's services for the Millbrook Medical Clinic. She is a member of the American Nursing Association and the Millbrook Historical Society.

Mr. Branigan is the son of the late James D. and Kathleen Ryan Branigan. He is president of Branigan Cranberries, Inc., founded by his parents, and a director of Bittersweet Bogs, both family-held operations. He is a graduate of Millbrook High School and Plymouth State Agricultural College.

Mr. Branigan is a member of the Friends of the Plymouth Philharmonic Orchestra, the Millbrook Country Club and the Plymouth County Cranberry Growers Association.

A July wedding is planned.

"A July wedding is planned," Bridget O'Connor muttered as she slid her sister's engagement announcement back into her purse and rifled through the rest of the contents. She'd meant to retrieve Erin's scribbled directions to Schuyler House on the Millbrook Common but *that* slip of paper appeared to be missing.

"On top of my dresser at the dorm, that's where I left them," she groaned. After glancing over the steering wheel to the highway rest area where she had parked, she slipped the car back into gear.

Undaunted, Bridget followed the highway to the Millbrook–Duxbury exit and then turned toward a single arrow pointing to Millbrook. Within moments she was winding her way west, away from the shore-line and over circuitous roads into the sand hills and pine forests of cranberry country. She was arriving from New Hampshire for the wedding, but it was only late April rather than July.

Her sister's discovery of impending motherhood had resulted in an abrupt change of wedding plans. Out went fair weather, tents at the country club and the buffer of myriad guests that might have made Bridget's misery less conspicuous. All that had been salvaged was the village church for the ceremony.

Now Bridget faced a private home reception and the intimacy of immediate family. Bridget O'Connor would no longer be able to disappear among the hordes. There would be scarcely anyone present for the weekend except O'Connors and Branigans.

For four interminable weeks she'd been nursing wounds left from her broken engagement. At twenty-two she'd sworn off fraternity weekends, blind dates and *Magnum P.I.* reruns. No hair of the dog for her. Bridget's resolve was steadfast. She wanted nothing to do with males of any description until calluses re-placed the blisters on her heart.

She intended to be tough—aloof and fancy-free. She was seven weeks from college graduation, with enough academic demands to fill even the most mo-rose moments. She was also ten weeks from her sis-ter's original wedding date. July would have suited her fine. By then she assumed her equilibrium might have returned and she would have been ready to face bach-elor ushers, bachelor friends and bachelor Branigans.

Bridget drove the back roads for twenty minutes before admitting to herself that she had no idea where she was. The landscape was open, beautiful and devoid of road signs. On her left she caught a glimpse of wide, rectangular bogs through the bare deciduous trees and spindly pines. At the opening to a lane fifty yards in front of her, she pulled over. Ancient Bancroft and Branigan placards were nailed to a maple trunk. She'd found the family compound. Someone would surely be on the grounds and could steer her toward the village center and Schuyler House. It was the home of Sky and Ryan Branigan and the place where all the O'Connors were staying for the wedding weekend.

Bridget turned onto the rutted lane and slowed as she reached a beautifully weathered Greek Revival house on the ridge. A profusion of daffodils lined the foundation. There were no cars in the gravel driveway so she continued down the hill to the house and barn complex that faced the open expanse of bogs. A compact car, a red Corvette and a panel truck lettered with Branigan Cranberries were parked in the courtyard.

She got out and stood looking at the maroon-colored expanse of working bogs dappled by the afternoon sun. Erin would be happy here, she thought. Despite the opinion of middle sister Megan, country living was in the O'Connor blood. Bridget was about to cross the courtyard and ask directions at the house when the squeak of the screen door made her turn.

She'd hoped for Kevin since he was the only Branigan she'd met. Instead a younger version of her sister's fiancé stepped onto the porch of the rambling farmhouse. Bridget took a deep breath, leaned back against her car and watched him with a jaundiced eye.

He could have been any one of the other five brothers—Drew, Sean, Ryan, Jody or Matthew. From that distance, age and eye color were indiscernible. This Branigan was an arresting physical combination of six-foot frame, square jaw, nutmeg-colored hair and fair complexion. It was a handsome combination and even from across the lawn he exuded confidence and determination. Bridget didn't give a fig for any male, but there was an unmistakable *something* about this one that set the warning flags waving the minute he stepped onto the porch.

He was most likely Ryan, Drew or Sean, one of the married brothers, she thought. Jody would be at his law office in Plymouth, and Matthew, the medical student, would be in Boston until the last minute.

A small spot under her ribs heated like toaster coils as he sauntered down the steps. It annoyed her. Bridget had no use for racing pulses or hammering hearts. Time would heal her wounds, not another man. If the merest glimpse of this one made her feel something besides numbness for the first time in weeks, she would only be that much more careful. It was irritating that she had to fight her own responses.

Whichever one he was, this Branigan's aloof, self-contained demeanor was apparent as he crossed the lawn. He was dressed as she was in faded jeans and a comfortable sweater, and he was deep in thought. A gust of wind caught his hair, and he rubbed his hands briskly against his arms. The reserve in his expression made him appear preoccupied. She watched his long, purposeful strides.

When he reached the paved courtyard, he caught sight of her and looked startled. *Delighted* or *infatuated* or *intrigued* might have helped sooth her shredded self-image. Nevertheless, he did smile. Bridget stepped away from her car and as his smile deepened, her mood softened.

"Hello," he called as he approached her.

She waited for him to get within speaking distance. "Hello. Would you be Drew Branigan?" She looked into his curious expression.

He shook his head. "Sorry. House up on the hill. I'm not sure he's home at the moment."

"Sean?" Gray-green. His eyes were gray-green and his lashes were thick.

"Nope."

"Ryan?" The glance between them held a moment too long. When he finally moved his gaze from her eyes, it was to look at the freckles that washed the bridge of her nose. "Jody, Matthew?" she added.

He laughed. "You forgot Kevin."

"I've met Kevin."

He looked across the crown of her tangled, flame-colored hair and said, "Which one would you like me to be?"

The ground seemed less firm beneath her moccasins. "One who can point me in the direction of Schuyler House."

He cocked his head. "Any one of us can do that. Take the lane back out to the county road. Turn right, then left at the crossroads. That'll take you into the village. The fire station will be on your right."

"I don't suppose you're the fire fighter?"

"That would be Sean."

"How about the identical twin?"

"Sorry. That's Drew."

"The house on the hill," she repeated. "Never mind. I'll be on my way. Schuyler House is halfway down Main Street?"

"Yes. Big white Colonial, directly across the common from the church. Look for Sky's old Mercedes in the driveway, or Ryan's Bronco."

"Thanks. Then you're not Ryan, either." She hadn't intended to enjoy this.

His smile was still broad. "Wrong again."

"That leaves the environmental lawyer and the bride's ex-roommate. I'm going to quit while I'm ahead.

He raised his eyebrows. "Any particular reason?"

Because it's time to hit the brakes. "It adds to the Branigan mystique," she replied, hoping she sounded witty.

"How about the O'Connor mystique? Are you going to tell me which one you are?"

"O'Connor? What makes you think I'm an O'Connor? Maybe I'm just a delivery service with wedding presents for Schuyler House."

"Not with your coloring," he said, glancing again at her blue eyes. The shell of her ears began to burn as he looked over at the rear of her car. "Not to mention the Barrett College decal on your rear windshield and the New Jersey license plate."

She offered her hand and laughed. "I'm Bridget, of course."

He shook it. "Of course."

They stared at each other again and the bachelor Branigan opened his arms. "We can do better than a handshake! We'll be family as of tomorrow." The hug was spontaneous. Bridget was five feet, seven inches tall, as lean and athletic as he was. She hadn't been held by anyone in weeks and this embrace was a perfect fit. For a split second her arms were slack from surprise, then she closed them around his back.

"Welcome to Millbrook, Bridget," he said at her temple.

Her "thank you" sounded absurdly weak. When he'd let her go, she pushed aside her short hair and tried to smile back at him. She was breathless and not a little confused. "Who, exactly, am I hugging— thanking—that is?"

"Jody's at his office."

"Then you must be Matthew." The softness of the vowels turned her pronunciation to a whisper.

"That I am." He looked startled again, as if he, too, needed to clear his head.

She turned away, to the open acres. "How appropriate that my first glimpse of Millbrook, Massachusetts, should be the Branigan cranberry bogs."

Matt swung his arm to encompass the view. "Feast your eyes."

I have popped into her head but she dismissed it. "Lots to see."

"Mostly maintenance and cultivation this time of year."

The late April weather had begun to add a touch of green to the acres of low, crimson bushes laid in the wide, rectangular bogs. Beyond them bare sugar maples and white-barked birches were framed by thick stands of pines.

"It's as beautiful as Erin's descriptions."

"We think so."

The open landscape was broken only by the houses of the oldest brothers, so often described by Erin. Drew and Holly's on the hill, Sean and Anne's across the irrigation pond. Bridget looked from them to the farmhouse behind Matt. "The homestead."

"Kevin and Erin's now," Matt added as he looked at the house he'd grown up in.

To Bridget he sounded wistful. "She'll make some changes."

"The O'Connor taste is welcome. There hasn't been a woman's touch in the house in twenty years, not since my parents died."

"Erin's told me."

"Of course." He gave her a noncommittal expression and checked his watch. The flirtatious atmosphere dissipated.

Bridget put up her hands. "Please don't let me interrupt. Erin said you were so busy you might not arrive until tomorrow. That's why I wasn't sure which brother you were."

"I managed to break away and bring work with me. In fact, I met your father's plane at the airport. We drove down from Boston together."

"Nevertheless, I'm sure Erin would give me strict instructions not to interrupt you."

"Your sister's still looking out for my welfare, after all this time."

Bridget searched his features for a hint of his own pain or a touch of regret. "Does that bother you?"

Matt glanced at the bogs. "I'd never have gotten this far without *somebody* breathing down my neck. I can't think of a thing about Erin that bothers me. Looking out for others is part of her nature. Kevin's too."

"How well I know" Bridget whispered. "Just to keep her happy, you mustn't tell anyone we've talked."

Matt's laugh did his face a world of good. "It's true you've caught me at a bad time, but feel free to roam around. I hate to run, but I've got to get back to work. I just came out to get a medical journal I left in my car. When you leave, follow the lane. Remember the rest?"

"Certainly. I'll know the house when I see it. Erin's described all of Millbrook a thousand times."

"She's described you that many times, too, Bridget. Make yourself at home. The bride's expecting you at Schuyler House. It's easy to find."

The bride. The tone in his voice had changed and she assumed she was meant to be going, but she couldn't ignore the currents that surrounded them.

"I'm on my way." It was an appropriate place to finish the conversation but she took a breath, not ready to leave just yet. "What are we competing with?"

He looked bemused. "At the moment, the end of my pediatric rotation."

"Medicine's a demanding mistress," Bridget replied.

"Pretty apt description. Except it doesn't keep me warm at night."

Surprise widened her eyes. Half a dozen witty replies filled her head but she kept them there as Matt added a goodbye and started back for the house. Bridget looked back out at the bogs and, after a moment's hesitation, began to walk along the bordering cart path. The April wind was brisk on the open land and she put her face to it as she strolled.

A year and a half earlier Bridget had been a college sophmore when her eldest sister had finished graduate school and moved to Boston. The Back Bay town house was full of serious graduate students, and Erin had moved into the fifth floor apartment her college friend Nancy Reed shared platonically with Matthew Branigan. They were both third-year Harvard Medical School students.

The life-style sounded ideal to Bridget, who considered herself removed from "Real Life" by the isolation of her New Hampshire campus. Bridget had a penchant for fleeting crushes, and the more Erin spoke of Matthew, the more he filled the bill.

However, at every opportunity Erin had lectured hard on the folly of falling for anyone studying to be a physician. "He wouldn't eat if I didn't feed him or pay the rent if I didn't mail the check. He doesn't have time to sleep, let alone date."

"Sour grapes?"

Erin had laughed. "Not a chance. Matt's a wonderful friend, but that's as far as it goes—for either of us."

"How about Nancy and Matt?"

"Medicine is enough to fulfill both of them. It has to be or they'd never survive Harvard."

"Then you shouldn't object if I want you to fix me up with him just for fun. I'll come down for a weekend."

"You?"

"What's that supposed to mean!"

"I don't want you starting off with someone like Matt."

"There *is* something between the two of you."

"There isn't. There can't be. Not for you, either, Bridget. Your campus is an hour and a half away. Women from here to Millbrook have stayed up nights wondering why he never called a second time. It never occurs to them that it's this crazy profession, not something they've done or haven't done."

The following weeks had proved her point. When Bridget had finally made it to Boston for a weekend, Matt was buried under his schedule and never left the hospital. Nevertheless Bridget envied the private jokes and small intimacies Erin seemed to share with him, as well as the apparent evidence of his gratitude for her attention. Their relationship may have been platonic, but it was close and loving and filled Bridget with longing. Matthew Branigan may have been absent from the apartment, but he became the subject of impossible fantasies, none the less.

After yet another conversation about her sister's elusive apartmentmate, Bridget had commented to Erin that he didn't seem like the heart-breaking type.

"He's the most dangerous kind. He's a natural flirt and he's oblivious to his effect on women. If you accused him of it, he'd simply laugh it off and not believe you. Trust me, medicine's the only mistress Matt wants and the only one he can handle. He's got another year of this grind, then internship and residency. Stick to the UNH and Dartmouth boys, or better yet, your books. The last thing you need is a broken heart."

Because she'd had no choice, Bridget had done just that. She'd put fantasies of Matthew aside, found the man of her dreams at Dartmouth in Todd Harrison and suffered a shattered heart anyway. Her chest ached now and she pressed her fist against her ribs as she walked along the edge of the bogs by herself.

First impressions were powerful. Matthew Branigan, flesh and blood at last, had more than lived up to her schoolgirl fantasies, but it no longer mattered. After much soul-searching, she was bound for Atlanta, Georgia, following graduation, bound and determined to start her professional life with a clean slate, free of encumbrances of the male variety.

Two

The brief Friday evening wedding rehearsal in the white clapboard church across the common from Schuyler House was only for the small wedding party. Bridget was already at the Millbrook Country Club for dinner when Matt, who was serving as best man for his brother, arrived with the rest of the attendants. She was standing at the fireplace of the private upstairs suite in low-heeled patent leather shoes. Her long legs shone in sheer, glittery hose, and her open-collared, emerald-green dress stopped above her knees. The wild, sophisticated curls around her face softened her features.

She was between conversations. After having listened to Nancy Reed's plan to begin her medical internship in London and her disdain of marriage, Bridget was left trying not to dwell on the fact that she'd had wedding plans of her own. She was a stranger to most of the men and women surrounding her and the more they teased and saluted Kevin and Erin, the more isolated she felt. She was making a valiant effort to put her own problems aside, but emotion had a way of welling up and dissolving her fortitude no matter how hard she worked at ignoring it.

The sudden sensation of a hand at her back broke her reverie. "Are you surviving all this family?"

Bridget turned and smiled bravely. "Ah, the best man."

Matthew smiled back. "We outnumber O'Connors by two to one tonight. I hope it's not too much for you."

"No more than for Erin."

"Good. I've been assigned to see that you enjoy yourself."

"Groom's orders or bride's?"

"I'm not sure I meant that the way it sounded."

She glanced across the room at her sister Megan, who was greeting the second bachelor Branigan. "Did you and Jody draw straws? He got Megan and you wound up with me for the duration of the weekend?"

Matt sharpened his gaze. "It's not an unpleasant assignment, Bridget."

They were interrupted by Hugh O'Connor's brief welcoming speech. "That's my cue," Matt murmured when her father had finished.

Bridget stayed at the fireplace and watched Matthew as he lead the families through a series of toasts to Erin and Kevin. In spite of herself, she noticed the slightest change in his expression, the fit of his clothes, the light in his hair.

Hair of the dog, she thought. The spot under her ribs, the place sandpaper-rough, was warming up again as she listened to the warmth in his voice. It stoked unaccountable irritation in her. He was laughing, reminiscing for the gathered family about his hectic life with Nancy and Erin in their Marlborough Street apartment.

Though his tone was light and the teasing good-natured, the underlying affection was unmistakable. It was obvious that Erin had been good for Matt. To Bridget, they seemed a perfect couple. They had the same agrarian backgrounds, the same love of medicine and love of life. The realization that she might not be the only one in the room nursing a broken heart shocked her.

The suddenness of the revelation softened her irritation. The familiar pain blended with surprise, and she turned away, reaching for an hors d'oeuvre. Conversation resumed as the toasts were completed. As dinner was announced, Matt excused himself from Erin and Kevin and came back to Bridget.

"I enjoyed your toasts," she said honestly.

"You have a heck of a sister. I meant everything I said. Dinner's been announced. Look's like I'm your escort." He crooked his arm and waited. Bridget hesitated, trying to ignore her involuntary responses as she put her hand on his arm and walked into the adjoining dining room.

Hugh O'Connor and Kevin Branigan were at either end of the table with family dispersed between them.

Bridget's place card was between Jody's and Matt's. Dinner was leisurely and, as father of the bride and host, Hugh O'Connor entertained from the head of the table with anecdotes about life as a widower with three daughters on a working dairy farm.

Matt was quiet. Although Bridget was continuously conscious of his presence at her right, the immediate conversation was held by Jody, on her left, whom she hadn't met before. She talked with him at length about his career in environmental law and Branigan plans to expand the bogs. As dessert was being served, Megan and Nancy picked up the discussion from across the table and Bridget turned to her coffee.

Matthew passed her the cream and sugar. "I understand you're after a career in journalism."

"Something related to commercial writing, possibly advertising or fund-raising."

"You originally had plans to work in Boston after graduation. Wasn't Thompson Associates interested?"

"Are all O'Connor lives open books?"

"Erin talks about you, yes. Your sister's proud of you—worried, too."

"She doesn't need to worry just because my plans have changed. I'm sure she's told you I'm going to Atlanta at the end of the summer."

He looked at her with those deep, green eyes. "Job offers of Thompson's caliber are hard to come by fresh out of school. Boston's a big town, Bridget. There's room for an ex-fiancé and you, too."

Bridget glared down the table at the bride, but Erin remained oblivious. "I was only coming to Boston because I thought I was marrying a guy who'll be in graduate school at MIT."

"Todd somebody?"

"Todd somebody," she muttered in reply.

"MIT's in Cambridge. You'll have the Charles River between the two of you."

Bridget sipped her coffee and did little to hide her irritation. "Has Erin discussed my private life with the entire Branigan clan or did she just fill you in before I was assigned to you for the weekend?"

He winced. "Don't be too hard on her. Erin cares about you, Bridget. Trite as it sounds, all she wants is your happiness."

"I doubt I'd find much happiness in Boston, river or no river."

Matt shrugged. "You don't seem like the type to let a man ruin your career."

His words made her throat burn until she had to blink. Her vision blurred Matt's remorseful expression.

"I'm sorry. I was out of line," he whispered.

She shook her head. When she could trust her voice, she added, "Actually, I'm the one who should apologize. Please excuse my behavior. It's been a long day."

"An even longer winter," Matt added. Around them guests were getting to their feet. Once again, he took her arm. "The party's breaking up, this is the perfect time to get you home."

She pressed the bridge of her nose as composure returned. "That's not necessary. I came out here with Ryan and Sky."

"Unless you want to explain to them why you have tears in your eyes and grief in your expression, come with me."

"It isn't grief."

"You're questioning my diagnosis? Your symptoms are irrefutable," he replied as they left the table.

She smiled wanly and followed him. However, before they could escape, Kevin and Erin caught up to them and thanked Matt for the toasts. Kevin shook his hand and Erin threw her arms around him. "You're the best, best man a bride could ask for, Harvard." She looked at Bridget and back to Matthew. "Take good care of her this weekend."

"Erin, really," Bridget protested, color flooding her cheeks.

"I'm taking her home right now, just to keep her out of harm's way."

To clear away her own pain, Bridget looked at Matt's soulful expression. There was more than fatigue playing in his features. He stirred her curiosity as well as that small spot under her ribs. Her sister had been so adamant about what could—or couldn't—develop with Matthew Branigan. Hadn't it occurred to Erin that her exhausted, overworked, dedicated medical student apartmentmate might have been in love with her?

Kevin Branigan was rugged, rich, independent, and he had more than ten years of life and experience on his youngest brother. Bridget walked out to the car in silence and pondered the anguish she was sure Matthew must have had to endure while his eldest brother swept Erin right off her feet. No wonder he'd recognized the symptoms in her. Matthew Branigan—the most dangerous kind of heartbreaker, the oblivious kind—might very well be tending his own broken heart. Fate had twisted all their lives.

Not only was he giving Erin up to his brother, he was serving as the best man during the process. The wedding ceremony might be even tougher for him to get through than for Bridget, herself. Thinking about the condition of Matthew's heart kept her from focusing on her own.

"You don't really have to drive me back to Schuyler House. I know it's out of your way," she offered as they left the building.

"It's a pleasant break from pediatric gastroenterology." He turned to her once they were in the car. "I'm sorry I dredged up all that fiancé business. No matter what Erin thinks, it really is none of my business."

Bridget leaned back against the headrest. "I didn't mean to be rude. I thought I was over the tears. It's all behind me, honestly. *Grief* is the wrong word."

"Call it anything you want. Something in you has probably died, Bridget, but you'll heal. I shouldn't have dwelt on you giving up your job, but you don't seem like the type to let a broken romance ruin your career plans. O'Connors are tougher than that. You're young and just starting out and damned better off on your own than putting some guy through grad school who didn't appreciate what he had."

"I can have a career in plenty of places other than Boston."

"You'd like Boston. Your sister was happy there."

His words gave Bridget an odd sense of uneasy calm. She was relaxed in Matt's presence, more relaxed than she'd imagined she would be, more relaxed than was healthy.

They followed a string of Branigan cars as they wound their way from the club back into the village. Bridget changed the subject and talked about life at Valley View, embellishing many of the stories her father had told at dinner until Matt's face was flushed from laughing.

"You can't live with Erin and not hear about the cows. Lactating cows, she swears, are what got her interested in OB/GYN nursing," he added.

Bridget smiled. "I suppose it would be like living with you and not hearing about the bogs."

"It's in the blood, like it or not."

As they turned onto Main Street, which bordered the Millbrook Common, the Branigan car in front of them turned into the first driveway, three down from Schuyler House.

"That's the carriage house Erin's been renting."

Matt nodded in the dark. "And that's Jody and Megan in front of us."

"I suppose you know Megan's going to take it over now that she's been transferred to Plymouth."

"Can't hurt my brothers, having another O'Connor in their midst." He laughed suddenly. "You see, Bridget? You're not the only O'Connor sister whose life seems an open book."

"I'm not sure whether that cheers me up. I hope Millbrook's big enough for both Erin and Megan."

He stopped the car in front of Ryan and Sky's. "You redheads bring out the best in us."

Bridget didn't reply right away, and the silence was unsettling. Matt's features were highlighted by the bright gray light from the street lamps, but shadows blurred his expression. She took a breath. "Matthew?"

"Yes?"

"Are you still in love with Erin?"

Matt didn't laugh at Bridget's question, though she'd almost hoped he might. He simply shrugged and leaned back. "Love comes in many forms," he said quietly.

Suddenly, Bridget didn't want to know how he felt about Erin. His voice was too wistful. She didn't want Matt to look at her with those deep, green eyes and confess that he still loved her sister. She didn't want to face his grief.

"At first I was horrified."

"Never mind, Matt. It's none of my business."

"That's never stopped an O'Connor."

"Maybe it should."

"You can hardly blame me for misjudging Erin. I thought I knew what was best for her."

Bridget sighed. "She's the one who's always known what everybody else needed."

Matt glanced through the dark windshield. "Erin has enough to worry about in her own life."

"Do you mean the wedding tomorrow or her unexpected pregnancy?"

He looked pained. "Kevin and Erin's original wedding date in July would have been a heck of a lot more convenient than this," he said, changing the subject somewhat. "I would have already graduated and started my internship."

"I know what you mean. I've got my last paper due next week as well as an oral exam and résumés to send to Atlanta. July would have been better for all of us. I was supposed to come for the wedding and stay for a week. Kevin offered me the farmhouse while they were on their honeymoon."

"Erin is something else. How on earth she could get pregnant when one of her nursing specialties is family planning—"

"Unbridled passion, I expect."

Matt winced. "Bridget, you're even more outspoken than your sister."

"Isn't unbridled passion why you had that silly fight with Kevin on the Fourth of July?"

He laughed ruefully. "Erin brings out the worst in me, too. I nearly rearranged Kevin's jawline over his behavior with her."

He turned off the ignition and turned in his seat. Outside, muffled voices and the faint slam of car doors broke the stillness as the others traipsed into the house. "It was stupid."

Instinctively, Bridget leaned toward him and touched his arm. "True, but it was also chivalrous and flattering."

He laughed again. "Chivalrous, flattering and stupid. When did you hear about the Fourth of July fiasco?"

Bridget smiled at him. "When Erin brought Kevin to Valley View at Christmas."

"Kevin enjoyed that visit." There was an imperceptible pause. "Todd was with you, wasn't he?"

"Yes."

"Kevin *did* mention that the four of you talked about weddings." The car keys jangled in his fingers. "Let's get you inside. It's late."

Bridget watched him look at her. "It's all right, Matt. I'm not going to dissolve again."

"Tears are cathartic."

"I've had about all the catharsis I can stand."

"It still hurts. I won't pry anymore."

Bridget waited. "How are you and Kevin getting along now?"

"Fine."

"Kevin's quite a man."

"A hard act to follow."

Bridget looked at Matt's profile, so like his brother's. "He's very proud of you."

"I'd hate to think where any of us would be without his sacrifices."

He was watching her and she touched her hair self-consciously as she looked across the console into his shadowed eyes. His expression made her heart pound. "Matt?"

"I was thinking about tomorrow. Besides the fact that it's April and damned inconvenient, how do you feel about this marriage? Which of your sisters do you agree with?"

"Megan disapproves, but she's a worrier, that's all. Her goals are a lot different from Erin's. She never much liked being a farm girl. She's more the doctor-lawyer type. She thought Erin was, too."

"So did I." He shifted the focus of the conversation. "What about the youngest O'Connor?"

"Me? I want a career, but I'll always love the country. Holsteins are some of my dearest friends."

Matt laughed. "Then the O'Connor sisters are about as different from one another as the Branigans are."

"Yes, I suppose we are."

When they finally got out of the car, they walked in comfortable silence up to the broad, raised paneled front door. Bridget was smiling. "Thanks for everything."

"Even my misguided concern?"

"Almost everything. Good as it is, you can save the bedside manner for your patients. I suspect you'll make a wonderful doctor."

"Thank you."

She watched the lamplight play on his face. "I hope I haven't kept you too late."

Matt shook his head. "Not at all. It's been quite a while since I did anything purely social, family or otherwise."

"All work and no play—"

"—makes a physician out of a med student, Bridget. I'm sorry there won't be much waiting for you when you get back on campus Sunday."

She shrugged. "I wouldn't say that. There's a lot of work waiting up there."

"Then make the solitude work to your advantage. This might be the perfect time in your life to be alone."

"I'm sorry Erin's discussed so much of my personal life."

"Don't be. It's only out of concern."

"As you said, she's got enough to worry about in her own life."

He was close to her now, his face bathed in the light from the porch lamp. Bridget was surprised at the lingering concern in his expression. "Let me know if I can do anything to help. How about tomorrow? Sitting through a wedding isn't the best prescription for healing a broken heart."

"I'm tougher than I look."

"Aren't we all?"

"Might the expression 'Physician, heal thyself' be appropriate?"

He looked thoughtful for a moment. "If you're referring to your sister, I admit, there was a time when I tried to imagine a relationship with Erin." He looked over Bridget's shoulder to the darkened common.

Bridget waited. "And?"

"It would have ruined a perfectly good friendship. I don't know the first thing about love. I don't have the energy to pursue it or the time to study it."

"You make it sound like an exotic disease."

"At this stage of my life, I know more about those. Your sister's always accusing me of knowing nothing about women's feelings. I was raised by five brothers and Peter Bancroft. I'm hardly to blame." He yawned and apologized.

Erin was dead wrong about that, but Bridget wasn't about to mention it. "Go home and get some sleep," she said instead.

"I've got a few hours of studying ahead of me first."

"Do you always run yourself ragged?"

"It'll be worse once my internship begins."

"Worth it, I hope."

"It's all I've ever wanted."

"Do you know what you want to specialize in?"

"Obstetrics, or maybe pediatrics."

"You may never sleep again!"

He laughed and stifled another yawn. "You may be right. Go on inside. I'll see you tomorrow, Erin."

Matt's slip of the tongue stabbed, but she treated it lightly. "Are you sure you know which O'Connor I am? You just called me Erin."

He blanched and Bridget laughed at his chagrin. "Erin's the bride. I'm the one you hugged this afternoon."

"Maybe I'd better make sure," he replied, suddenly sly.

His playfulness startled her. Before she could catch her breath, he wrapped his arms around her. "You do feel like the one I hugged this afternoon. You must be Bridget."

This time the hug wasn't buffered by heavy sweaters and denim. He caught her off balance and tightened his grasp when she slipped. With her arms still at her side, Bridget shifted from one foot to the other and her thighs pressed against the thin fabric of the dress slacks wrapping his hips. She raised her arms across the breadth of his shoulders and felt the strength of his arms, the solid wall of back. Every one of his muscles hardened against her softness as her breasts molded against his chest.

He took a sharp breath. "You're Bridget, no doubt about it." His complexion was flushed and the gray-green of his eyes had darkened to smoke. "I'm not likely to make that mistake again." He stepped back as if to let her go but instead opened his fingers in the tangle of her hair. "Hell," he muttered, "I've wanted to do this since I watched you walk the bogs."

Any semblance of a laugh caught in her throat as he leaned forward and brushed her lips. His were incredibly warm, firm, sensuous in ways she'd fantasized about so long ago. Her body ached to respond but her intellect wouldn't allow it.

They parted and Matthew touched her cheek. "That was out of line. Forgive me."

"It was nice. There's no need to apologize."

"Then I'll just say good-night. Sleep well, Bridget."

He walked into the night and she stayed on the granite stoop until his car had disappeared down the street. Before she went inside she tried to clear her head, tried to keep her lips from tingling and her body from aching. She tired not to think about the image of Matthew Branigan watching her from his homestead as she'd walked the dike along his bogs that afternoon.

Bridget's father, Hugh, as well as Erin and Kevin, was in the Schuyler House library with Ryan and Sky Branigan. They were discussing Megan O'Connor's move to Millbrook while they waited for Jody to bring her home. Bridget joined the group long enough not to appear rude, then went upstairs to her room.

She was sharing it with her middle sister and had intended to discuss Megan's misgivings about the marriage. That was before she'd arrived in the picturesque town, before she'd watched the Branigan men en masse, before Matthew had held her in his arms. She no longer wanted to talk about Branigans—any one of them. Kevin and Erin belonged together and whatever Megan was up to with Jody was her business.

As for her own convoluted circumstances, she kept telling herself the kiss was nothing. Compassion was part of Matthew's nature—his career. She neither needed nor wanted the feelings, he invoked. She was only his assignment for the weekend. It was only a hug. Well, two hugs and a kiss. Bridget left a single lamp on and got into bed.

Three

The wedding ceremony was beautiful in its simplicity. Other than immediate family, guests included only Nancy Reed and a few friends and associates. They all gathered in front pews of the little church to witness the vows.

As maid of honor, Megan O'Connor walked from the sacristy to the altar with the Branigan children, Maria, Suzanne and Kate, who carried baskets of lilies that matched the yellow of their dresses. Bridget watched with a lump in her throat and finally glanced at the best man.

Physically, there was little contrast between the groom and Matthew. Twelve years separated the eldest from the youngest, but they shared the striking Branigan features that were the hallmarks of each of the brothers. Kevin was known for his pragmatism and stoic determination. Matt had inherited a good deal of those traits, as well, tempered, as Bridget had witnessed, by compassion.

The bridal couple began to exchange vows. She watched Matt as he smiled at Erin. Kevin began to speak, then stopped, at a loss for words. Matt put his arm on his brother's shoulder, but Kevin's voice still faltered. Bridget could hear the break in his voice. Matt handed him a handkerchief, which Kevin pressed unceremoniously to his eyes. The lump in Bridget's throat burned and next to her in the pew, Drew chuckled softly. "Will you look at that! The bigger they are, the harder they fall."

Schuyler House was the perfect size for the reception. Its gracious rooms held the family and guests comfortably. After toasts and good-natured teasing about Kevin's emotions, everyone mingled in the parlor, dining room and library.

"Did you survive the ceremony?"

Bridget turned to find Matt behind her. "I think I held up better than the groom."

"Kevin beats everything. At one point, I thought I'd have to hold him up. Erin's brought out a side he's kept hidden a long time." Matt looked at her analytically. "How about you, Bridget? Has the day been too painful?"

"No. I'm fine."

Matt waited.

"Really. I'd like to put my whole pitiful, ridiculous romance behind me. It wasn't meant to be and I'm lucky I found out when I did."

"Then don't let a broken engagement change your career plans."

Bridget couldn't help but glare. "There's nothing more to talk about. Please don't lecture."

He smiled. "Branigans love to lecture. Let me be the first to point out that now you have six big brothers—"

"*In-law*, Matthew," she interrupted, "with their own lives to run. I don't need any one of them giving me career guidance."

As she finished, Matt tucked his elbow through hers. "That remains to be seen," he added as he steered her from the crowded parlor. She glanced for help from either sister, but Erin was posing for photographs and Megan was occupied with Jody. Bridget wound up in the empty foyer. "There's nothing waiting for you in Atlanta but a vacant bedroom in a crowded apartment."

She leaned back against the bannister and considered the green of his eyes. "You've shared apartments, too. I'll have friends in Atlanta."

"You have *family* here and a secure job offer with a great future."

"I've already told Thompson Associates that I've changed my mind about their offer. I don't have a job in Boston and I intend to find one in Atlanta."

"Starter salary will make airfare home awfully tight, and it's a heck of a drive from Georgia to New Jersey when you get a hankering for a Holstein."

Bridget fought a smile and sank onto the stair riser. "Dr. Branigan, I don't want your advice."

Matt sat down next to her. "I've got five brothers and you've got two sisters in this house—if you don't like my advice, go get a second opinion. I doubt you'll be any better off."

Emotion tightened her throat again and she had to choose her words carefully. "I don't want a second opinion."

"Afraid that someone might agree with me?"

"Matthew, please. I've worked it all out. I'll be starting over, can't you see that? Atlanta's a clean slate, a fresh start away from everything."

"*Everything* is the operative word, Bridget. Away from Todd, yes, but you're cutting out everybody who loves you and the work you wanted so badly just to escape a broken heart."

"You're sounding like my father." She stood up.

Matt tugged her gently by the wrist until she sat back down. "Hugh's concern is well-founded. So is Erin's. It doesn't take the entire length of the East Coast to buffer and heal a broken heart."

"Sorry, Doctor, this is one illness you're not familiar with. You said so yourself."

Suddenly, his authoritative tone softened. "Your fiancé broke the engagement. Are you so devastated that you'd give up your own dreams to be rid of the nightmare of losing Todd?"

She stared hard, straight ahead, across the foyer to the closed front door. Her ears burned and her throat was constricted. Because of Todd she was numb, but because of Matthew Branigan she was confused. His lecturing angered her, but the undeniable undercurrent of something else deepened her skittishness. "I need the distance."

The intimacy in his voice made her ache. "Bridget, through all the drudgery of medical school, all these years of studying, the one thing that's kept me sane has been my family. I've had Millbrook as a refuge and everybody in these rooms to lean on when things got rough."

"I won't have that kind of pressure," she replied through pursed lips.

He looked at her carefully. "You already have. Why do you think I know about you and Todd? Because when the going got rough you turned to your family, and in a convoluted way that's included me."

"It shouldn't."

He touched her hand. "You asked me if I was in love with Erin."

"It's none of my business."

"It was a fair question and the answer is yes. Not the way you loved Todd, certainly, but she gave me a woman's perspective, a sister's almost. After twenty years of male households, I love her for it. I always will. The reverse is true, too. She's shared her problems with us, especially when she's needed a man's perspective."

"Are you telling me she needed a man's opinion on what to do about poor little Bridget? *Male* opinions are not appreciated. Sorry."

"Erin's part of your life and Megan will be right here, too."

"Did it ever occur to you that I want to get away from my sisters' influence? I need to be on my own, to make my own mistakes and take care of my own tragedies. You're sounding an awful lot like one of them.''

''Bridget—''

She turned her unfocused stare on Matt. ''Wait a minute. Erin put you up to this, didn't she?'' When color mottled his complexion, she smirked. ''You don't even have to answer, Dr. Branigan. It's written all over your face. Erin doesn't want me so far away— my father doesn't, either. They want me where they can manipulate me and Georgia's just too darn far! I can't believe they talked you into mediating!'' The look in his eyes made her suddenly self-conscious and she stood up. ''Thanks for the lecture but I don't need your altruism. The sister of the bride will be just fine.''

''Bridget, stay here.''

She shook her head. ''Not here on the stairs and not in Boston. Sorry, Matt. I know what's best for me. Tell Erin you gave it your best shot. We O'Connors can be every bit as stubborn as Branigans.''

Thankfully, dinner was announced and with that, Bridget went into the dining room. She was hurt and she ached with embarrassment. How absurd to think Matt's interest had been anything more than a reflection of her sister's misplaced concern. She felt foolish and that made her cheeks burn.

She paused and leaned over as she passed behind Erin's chair. ''Matt's done your bidding. I appreciate your concern, but you have enough to worry about in your own life. Stay out of mine, big sister.''

Erin pivoted in her seat and raised her eyebrows. ''You've been talking with Matt?''

"Listening mostly."

"I hope he can talk some sense into you."

"He gave me your point of view."

"Bridge—"

She put her hand on her sister's shoulder. "Erin, you've mothered and smothered me since we were kids. Let me make my own mistakes."

"You already have and Atlanta will just be another."

"Not as big as loving Todd Harrison."

"It might be." The voice was low, male and by now, familiar. As Bridget spun around to face Matt, he pulled out a chair and waited for her.

"No, thank you. I'll sit across the table."

In reply, he pointed to the place cards above the dinner plates. *Bridget O'Connor* in neat, black calligraphy was next to *Matthew Branigan.*

When they'd sat down, he leaned over. "It was my kiss, wasn't it."

"What?"

"I kissed you last night. You kissed me back. We've been too intimate. You swore you'd never kiss another man and you did. Now you're running off to Atlanta to hide."

"How can you joke?" she sputtered.

"Because high melodrama isn't my style and I hope to heaven it isn't yours. Not when there's so much at stake."

"Matthew Branigan, let me enjoy my dinner." She took a bite of salad and chewed, all the while feeling his stare. "For all I know, my sisters instructed you to kiss me."

He raised his eyebrows. "As long as I was lecturing, you mean? The thought's flattering, but not the O'Connor style, I'm afraid. I thought of the kiss all by myself. After the demands of medical school, it was a relief that I remembered how."

"You *are* turning this into a joke."

He turned to his own plate. "It was worth a try. I didn't get very far being serious. I only kissed you because you're moving to Atlanta and you'll need a point of reference—Yankees as compared to Southerners. I never would have considered it if I thought you might change your mind and stay up here."

"Well, my goodness, you should have made that clear. My response was hardly my best effort." With that Bridget turned in her chair and chatted with Ryan, seated on the other side of her.

The mood was festive and the air of celebration carried the meal. There was enough conversation and anecdotes from the rest of the guests to keep more intimate reprimands at bay. Bridget made a concerted effort to enjoy herself and much to her surprise, Matt didn't mention the kiss again, keeping the conversation light. Neither of them was about to spoil the day.

After throwing the bouquet from the staircase—into the arms of Kate Branigan, hoisted into the air by her father, Sean—Erin prepared to leave for her abbreviated honeymoon. Bridget hugged her sister. "It was a beautiful day, Mrs. Branigan."

Erin put her at arm's length. "Even with all the advice?"

"Well-intentioned."

"And in the end, you'll do just what you think's best. I suppose that's the way it ought to be."

"It's what you've done, Erin."

She turned and smiled at Kevin. "So it is. We'll be up to see you graduate in a few weeks, and no matter where you decide to settle, we still expect you for some vacation here in June."

"Now that I've seen the bogs and Millbrook, I think that much is a great idea."

"Wonderful! Behave yourself till then. Get through your finals and we'll celebrate at the bogs."

Twenty minutes after Kevin and Erin had gone, Bridget was in the butler's pantry looking for plastic wrap to save little Maria Branigan's slice of wedding cake. Matt appeared in the doorway. "I didn't want to leave without saying goodbye."

"You're leaving?"

He smiled at her surprise. "Now there's an expression that does my heart good. I have a long night ahead of me and some patients I want to check on."

"Of course." She ignored the stab of disappointment.

"Ryan's driving Megan and your dad to the airport in the morning. I assume you'll be heading back to campus after breakfast."

She nodded. "Lots of work ahead of me, too."

"Good luck, then."

"Same to you, Matt."

"Pass along all your news to Erin so she can keep me posted. Even though that's half the reason you're running away to Georgia."

"We've finished talking about my reasons for moving to Atlanta." She was standing with her back to the counter and cabinets.

"I was hard on you," he added.

"It's all right. You were only telling me what Erin wanted me to hear."

"You know your own heart, Bridget. Erin will have to accept it."

"Then you agree with me." She looked up at him. It was the same look as their first, a challenging gaze between blue eyes and green that burned with anticipation. Inexplicably her heart began to pound as she waited for him to respond.

He took the box of wrap out of her hand and put it on the countertop beside him. "What I think won't change your mind. What I want won't, either."

The pounding increased. "What *do* you want, Matt?"

"Your best effort." There was pressure at her back, a wide warmth where Matt opened his own hand as he leaned gently against her. The heat grew to a glow that expanded as it fanned into the recesses of her throat, through her chest and the hardening tips of her breasts and down into her hips.

The thunder of her pulse made her breath catch. She felt the bristle of his hair against her palm before she realized she had her hand behind his head. She tried not to respond, not to melt against him, but when Matt closed his eyes and pressed his mouth against hers, she welcomed him. The kiss was tortuously sweet, tinged with her sigh. He traced her lips with his tongue until she moaned softly. He cupped her face, plundered her mouth, and in one flash of eroticism, Bridget imagined them somewhere else, alone, for the moment. Matt's grip tightened as his own breath caught in his chest.

Desire for him overpowered her as if it were some primal signal that her heart would heal, that she would feel whole again in someone else's arms. But Matthew Branigan? The family circumstances, the brevity of their friendship, *the butler's pantry*, for heaven's sake—all of it was enough to add an undercurrent of fear.

Matt's caress grew unbearably sensuous as he responded to her. Her body ached to encourage him even as she fought to remind herself where she was, *who* he was. Fear for her heart drowned the desire in the moment of panic and she put both hands against his chest.

"Matt!"

Immediately he moved his hands from her face to the countertop on either side of her.

Bridget pulled back, panting. Her life was chaotic enough without these complications, these feeling for a man—any man—but especially a Branigan who knew far too much about her already.

"Matt, please. This is crazy."

He closed his eyes until composure returned and then traced her jaw with his thumb. The sensation shot through her and she trembled. "That's a relief. I was afraid after a kiss like that, you'd call me Todd."

"You're nothing like Todd."

"Then it *was* me you were kissing."

"I shouldn't have, and I'd appreciate it if you wouldn't mention it. I doubt anyone here has an ounce of discretion."

"That wasn't necessary," he muttered.

She regretted it, but didn't apologize. She was desperate for emotional distance between herself and the youngest Branigan.

Four

———

May on the Barrett College campus passed in a blur of cramming for final exams, the packing of four years' worth of accumulated memorabilia and preparation for "Real Life." Bridget's closest friends were scattering for the summer and the Atlanta contingent was delighted that she would join them at the end of August. The only frustration was the lack of response from Atlanta businesses to whom she'd sent her résumé.

The memory of her responses to Matthew Branigan's kisses still raced her pulse, but it served as a reminder that there were lots of fish in the sea—when, and if, she was ready for another romance. By the middle of the month, Bridget had received a stack of rejections from her unsolicited attempts to interest Georgia firms in a green college graduate and it was getting harder to maintain her resolve. Of course, she would have friends there and enough savings to get her through the first few months of shared apartment rentals and communal food shopping. As graduation approached, she worked at convincing herself that opportunity would present itself once she pounded the pavement in person.

Erin kept her informed about life in Millbrook. Megan's business transfer came through and she moved from New Jersey to the carriage house, taking over the public service position at WJQG, the Plymouth radio station. Erin talked of Holly's pregnancy, the legal entanglements of reopening the old bogs on neighboring Taft property, Kate's bout with the chicken pox and the conversion of Jody's old bedroom into a nursery for her own expected child. The biggest news, however, was Megan's tempestuous relationship with Jody, which Branigans and O'Connors were now discovering had started long before the wedding weekend.

Protests aside, Bridget cared deeply about her sisters' lives. She found it amusing that now so much of their news was about one or another of the Branigan men. Matt had been right about one thing. There would be a certain amount of homesickness associated with Atlanta. Still, she needed distance from more than an ex-fiancé. Didn't she?

The day before graduation, Bridget picked up the last of her mail. Todd sent her a graduation card, which she read at her mailbox. Guilt dripped from his kind words and best wishes. It was thoughtful, she had to admit, but remnants of her heartache stabbed at her. She tossed the card in the junk mail barrel before she left the student union.

The remaining envelope stopped her as she crossed the campus. Matt Branigan had sent a note that included a hand-drawn caricature. He'd drawn a well-endowed Southern Belle standing by the side of a road. The cartoon character was hitchhiking in full antebellum garb and she had short, curly, flaming red hair. Her suitcase had a Barrett College pennant on the side. Atlanta or Bust dangled from a banner in her hand. Bridget's heartache dissolved as she looked it over. Scribbled across the bottom was:

While you're sipping mint juleps and setting Atlanta on fire (again), think of the struggling intern in the frozen north.

The best of everything, Bridget. Here's to a bright future.

Cheers, from all the Branigans,
Matt

Bridget looked at the trees overhead and out to the brick-front sorority houses. Since the day she'd returned to campus, she'd been trying to put thoughts of Matthew Branigan aside, at least the lurid, unsolicited thoughts that had kept the remembrance of their moments in the butler's pantry so vivid. She folded the note and put it in her purse. He was graduating, too, and had far more to be proud of than she. She reversed her path and headed back for the student union bookstore in order to buy him a card, one devoid of any intimacy.

Life kicked into double time. Hugh O'Connor flew to New Hampshire for graduation in order to help his daughter with the eight-hour drive home to Valley View. Megan O'Connor drove from Millbrook with Kevin and Erin for the day. She was tight-lipped about her relationship with Jody as Kevin discussed his brother's startling plans to give up his law practice in order to join the family cranberry business.

Amidst hugs, tears and promises to keep in touch, Bridget and her classmates said goodbye to one another. She made sure to introduce the three Atlanta-bound women to her family and, armed with a bachelor's degree in Journalism, Bridget left the hallowed halls of Barrett College for Women.

She spent her first week as a graduate at home in New Jersey, putting in long hours at the dairy with her father. She unpacked, sorted through her memorabilia and waited in vain for the ultimate job offer from Atlanta. At the end of the month she accepted Erin's invitation and prepared to set out on the road again, this time for a vacation at the bogs. The day before her departure, a forwarded piece of mail arrived from Boston by way of the college.

Back Bay Associates was a fund-raising firm with a national reputation recommended to her in March by the Alumni Office. BBA president Hilary Brooks and chief account executive Carla Benoit were both Barrett graduates from the sixties. Even though it was networking and Bridget had then been determined to set Boston, not Atlanta, on fire, she hadn't held out much hope for a reply of any sort from such a prestigious firm.

The brief letter was from Carla Benoit. Business had kept her out of town and she'd just gotten to Bridget's letter. She thanked her for her résumé, was honest about not having anything available at the moment, but if Bridget were still interested, suggested an interview as soon as possible.

Bridget chose not to mention the letter to her father. She felt ambivalent at best, held little hope of being hired even with an interview and didn't want the inevitable fatherly advice. "Atlanta," she whispered out loud. She would sooner wait tables or deliver pizza in Atlanta than develop a career in Boston. Still it *was* Back Bay Associates.

Inertia kept her out at the mailbox while she mulled over the offer. If Todd had still been in her life—she forced herself not to think of Todd. Instead, Matt's words filled her head. *Was she so devastated by a mere man that she'd throw away her entire career in Boston?*

Bridget shut her eyes, damning the small *yes* floating in her head. Just to spite her ex-fiancé she went into the house and picked up the phone. By the time she'd hung up, she'd arranged a Tuesday-morning interview at Back Bay Associates. Carla Benoit would see her personally.

The following afternoon, after a seven-hour drive, Bridget found the Millbrook homestead easily. The New England landscape had greened since the chilly April weekend and the Branigan acres were now sheltered from the roads by thick foliage. Trucks were in the barn, dogs were barking and a lawn tractor was being driven as she pulled her car up next to Kevin's Corvette.

The air was sweet with the scents of honeysuckle and freshly mown grass. Beyond the courtyard the pond glistened and the gardens were blooming in the late-Monday sun. Kevin, with one retriever at his heels, was out along the far edge of the property tinkering with the irrigation system.

As in April, the sound of the screen door made Bridget turn. This time it was Erin who came across the lawn to welcome her. Bridget hugged her sister, then put her at arm's length to take a look at the maternity jumper.

"I thought you might still be at work. You look more pregnant by the week!"

"I just got home. You should feel this little person kick! I hope you brought lots of old clothes. Kevin's got plans to put you to work in the garden. I get green around the gills at the smell of snow peas and spinach, which makes me useless out there."

"Raging hormones," Bridget replied, wagging her finger. "Of course that's what put you in this condition in the first place."

"This condition suits me fine. We intend to fill the house."

"Fill the house? Not six again, I hope!"

"Two at least. One for Kevin and one for me."

Bridget pulled her luggage from the trunk. "I bet Megan can hardly stand your being so domestic."

Erin rubbed her back. "Megan's out of sorts at the moment. She's got her own life to figure out. Don't expect her at any family gatherings while you're here.

The on-again, off-again with Jody is off, again. Believe it or not, *I'm* even trying to stay out of this one."

"She should have known being involved with a Branigan would put her in a fishbowl."

"Love makes you irrational."

"Is she in love with Jody?"

Erin shrugged. "Who can tell? How about you— feeling more human than you were in April?"

"I'm over Todd, if that's what you're hinting at."

"But it's still Atlanta, come hell or high water. Will you ever set foot in Boston?"

Bridget grabbed the opening and fibbed. "As a matter of fact, I thought I might run in tomorrow. The shops at Dean's Corner don't carry anything remotely resembling professional wardrobes. If I'm going to begin a career, I have to dress for success. Maybe I'll take in a few of the tourist attractions, too."

Erin picked up Bridget's small bag and they walked to the house. "Why not wait a few days till somebody can go with you? I have to work, but Sky might like to show you around. As a matter of fact, Matt—"

Bridget cut her off and continued the deception. "I'd really like to go alone. I don't want to feel rushed when I'm trying on clothes. I'd bore your in-laws to death." She opened the screen door and waited for Erin to enter. "Now tell me what I can do for you around here."

"I did mention that gardening, and Matt may need your help, too, if you're interested."

"Matt?" Bridget frowned at her sister's sly smile.

"I tried to tell you a minute ago. Matthew's just started his one and only vacation between med school and his internship. He and Jody own a boat they keep in Plymouth, and Matt's been tinkering on it this weekend."

"Is he staying in Plymouth at Jody's?" Bridget asked hopefully.

"Heaven's, no. Jody's all tied up with his business crisis and surviving his involvement with our sister."

Bridget paused. "What do you suppose the odds are that two O'Connor-Branigan relationships could survive?"

Erin smiled slowly. "With apologies to Holly, Sky and Annie, I'm just sorry there weren't six O'Connor sisters."

"Then you approve of Megan and Jody?"

"Megs doesn't need my approval. She's got enough to wrestle with in her own heart. Life around the bogs is jam-packed with surprises. As for you, just relax and enjoy yourself."

"I'm sure I will, as long as you hold off on the lectures. You still haven't told me where Matt's staying."

The eldest O'Connor grinned.

Bridget scowled. "Erin, he isn't staying here?"

"This is his home, Bridget."

"Why didn't you tell me?"

"Problem?"

"Of course not. I'm just surprised, that's all."

"Just the four of us. It'll be great fun."

"Weren't you the one who told me to steer clear of Matthew Branigan?"

"Back when you were interested in Matt you were a green college kid, Bridge. Todd Harrison toughened you up." Erin patted her shoulder. "Chalk it up to experience. Enjoy Matt's company while you're here. You can handle him."

"Thanks for the vote of confidence."

They went into the big country kitchen. "You know this is where I stayed for a week as Kevin's house guest. This wonderful house is where—"

"Erin, I know all about your falling in love with Kevin."

"Atmosphere is everything."

"Mixed signals, even from my own sister," Bridget muttered. "I should have stayed home with the Holsteins."

The women walked through the house and upstairs to the bedrooms. "Growing up, Ryan and Matt shared the one with the bunk beds. We've put you up in the front, next to us. Peter Bancroft had it for a time, next it was Drew's room, till he married Holly. By then Matt was in Boston and Ryan took over Drew's. It's where I stayed."

Bridget put her hands up. "Not another word about Branigan bedrooms!"

"Well at least come and see the nursery. Kevin's having more fun than I am getting it in shape." When the luggage was settled, Erin led the way back down the hall. "Nobody had done a thing with this house in years," she added as they opened the door to a cheerful, bright nursery. She pointed to the closet. "Kevin'll be working on that this week. He's custom designing shelves and a hanging system that can be adjusted as the baby grows.''

Bridget smiled as she looked at the walls. ''I thought for sure you'd stencil cranberries in here.''

In response, Erin unrolled a foot of wallpaper border. ''Farm animals, every fourth one is a Holstein!''

''Anybody home?''

The booming masculine voice rising up from the staircase made the women stop. ''In the nursery,'' Erin called.

Bridget turned around at the sound of footsteps, expecting Kevin. Instead Matt Branigan filled the doorframe.

Five

Matthew looked at Bridget as though nothing awkward had passed between them during the wedding weekend. He looked remarkably rested. High color in his cheeks from the sun as well as that engaging smile brightened his features. He'd shoved both hands into his jeans pockets and his rumpled work shirt lay open at the throat. She'd forgotten how expressive his eyes were.

"Welcome back," he said from the doorway. "I wasn't sure you'd ever return after the browbeating we gave you in April."

"I had no idea you'd be here," Bridget replied, trying to quell the intensity of her response.

"The honeymooners talked me into it."

Erin nodded. "You can't imagine how badly this

man needs some rest and relaxation away from the medical environment.''

Matt winked at Bridget. ''Didn't I tell you your sister's still watching out for my welfare?''

Erin shooed them from the room. ''Somebody has to. You're still incapable of eating more than one well-balanced meal a week.''

''Doctors live on adrenaline and caffeine, you know that.'' Matt crossed the hall to his own room, unbuttoning the rest of his shirt as he went. ''If you'll give me fifteen minutes to shower off the smell of teak oil and tidal mud, I'll come down and make scintillating conversation while you concentrate on my nutritional requirements.''

He began to strip off his shirt and paused before tossing it. ''Bridget, any chance you know how to balance a meal?''

''Of course.''

''I'm a sucker for O'Connor cooking.'' With that he threw the balled up fabric in the general direction of the clothes hamper in the open bathroom. When it fell short, he closed his door. Only Erin was left to see the bright flush that had settled across her sister's cheekbones. With the exception of the tour of the nursery, nothing was going as Bridget had expected.

Twenty minutes later Bridget was with the honeymooners on the farmer's porch, waiting for chicken to barbecue. Matt joined them at the grill. His hair was wet, and the hint of his after-shave wafted over the aroma of the chicken as he took the tongs from Kevin and turned each piece on the coals. ''There. Proof I can cook.''

"We keep him around so he can practice his surgical skill on carving our roasts," Kevin replied.

Bridget enjoyed the banter, grateful for the company. Matthew's presence was just as unsettling as she'd remembered. Or maybe it was what she remembered that made him so unsettling. He had a way of glancing at her that told her explicitly that he was remembering, too.

"Plans for tomorrow?"

"I'm going into Boston."

"You?"

"To shop," she lied. "I don't have much of a wardrobe for Atlanta."

"Still heading for the land of magnolias."

She narrowed her gaze. "I made my plans clear at the wedding."

"Clear as the sky over these bogs, Bridget. I wish you well."

"Thank you. Let's not bicker over it. Thanks for your card, by the way. You're very clever."

"I have my moments. Thank you for yours."

"Finishing medical school is a big step, Dr. Branigan." Bridget returned his gaze. "How long will you be staying here?"

"I've been here a week—one more to go."

"If there's time, I'd like to see your boat."

He wagged the tongs at her as he put the chicken on the platter. "I'm in the market for some elbow grease. If you feel like working, I'll reward you with a sail across the bay."

"I'll earn the sail, I assure you."

Matt smiled. "I'll see that you do."

Her heart jumped.

After dinner Megan arrived as Drew and Holly walked down the hill with their daughter. The extended family stayed out on the lawn bordering the bogs. On the pretext of needing the exercise, Erin called the dogs and set off along the cart path with Megan. Bridget felt Matt move next to her as she watched her sisters go.

"An O'Connor heart-to-heart?" he asked.

"I don't know and I'm not sure I want to."

"I got an earful in our apartment days. I'll have to admit, Erin's advice is usually sound. Funny thing, she's the youngest of all my sisters-in-law, but I can already see her as the matriarch of the family."

"It suits her."

"Suits Kevin, too, since he'll always rule the roost. There's a kind of comfort in that."

"Comfort?"

"Knowing somebody's in control, somebody's holding the threads that weave us all together."

Bridget looked out at the trees. "Matthew, I can't think of anyone in more control than you. Your whole life's in order."

"And that's what you're striving for, control? Order?"

"I envy your professional life."

"Yes, but remember, it doesn't keep me warm at night." She was still looking straight ahead as he added, "However, when the sun's gone down, I doubt you're any warmer than I am."

She turned to reply but the entire group was distracted by the crunch of tires on the gravel. A sleek

Porsche purred to a stop in the cobbled courtyard and Jody got out. He was far less animated than the last time Bridget had seen him. She wasn't the only one who watched as he went out to Megan and she turned to continue her walk. Bridget found nothing but pain in either face.

"Greetings, family," Jody added to the gawkers when he'd come back. "Holly, can you spare half an hour?"

The tense scenario dissolved as Holly responded and handed her daughter to Drew. The toddler kissed her mother from Drew's shoulders, and then Holly and Jody wandered up the hill to the house, already deep in discussion.

"Fishbowl," Bridget muttered.

The assembled O'Connors and Branigans finished the evening together. Erin went up to bed shortly after Drew took Maria home. Bridget was relieved that Matt went into the house with Kevin, having feared more innuendos. To make it clear to him that she wouldn't follow, she walked Megan to her car.

"I'm sorry you and Jody are having trouble."

"Jody's in the midst of a career crisis. He'll tell you himself the last thing he needs is a woman to worry about. I certainly don't need the pressure, either. I've got my own life to straighten out."

"Yours always was so orderly, Megs."

"Still is, little sister—yours should be, too. Just don't let a man dictate your decisions. Romance can be very fleeting, then you're stuck with empty dreams and stupid decisions."

"I'm one step ahead of you on that score. Besides, I've already had this lecture."

"Take it to heart. This Atlanta thing had better be right for you and not just to put Todd in the dust."

"We're talking about me? I thought for sure you meant yourself and the attorney." Bridget laughed. "'Todd in the dust,' I like the sound of that."

When they'd parted, Bridget stayed out on the lawn. The floodlight at the corner of the barn and the moon in the cool June sky threw enough light for her to see her way clearly. She'd pulled on a sweater at sunset and was grateful for it as she followed the cart path, as she had her first afternoon in Millbrook.

She'd reached the last dike that split the bogs when the sound of soft whistling made her stop. Over the constant croaking of peepers she listened, then turned and waited.

A Branigan, nearly in silhouette, was strolling over the path toward her. She stood still and her heart quickened as the moon revealed his face.

"I thought you were Kevin."

"He's gone to bed and I've been waiting for you."

"Waiting?"

"I'd like to clear the air between us, Bridget. Bring up what hasn't been mentioned since you arrived."

"Matthew—"

"I don't want to spend this vacation pretending nothing happened in the pantry last April."

"Nothing much *did* happen. It was just one of those things. I'm sure you've kissed lots of women in similar circumstances, and I can't imagine that you've apologized to them for it."

"I never felt the need before."

They walked slowly, matching each other's pace. "Sounds like home, we've got peepers, too." Bridget whispered, deliberately changing the subject. A bullfrog croaked, and she turned to the pond, inky under the stars. Her heart was still racing and as Matt's shoulder brushed hers, the sound of her pulse inside her head obliterated everything but its insistent rush.

"Cold?"

She shook her head.

"I can feel you trembling."

"I'm fine, really." She bent for a stone to throw in the water, and Matt knelt next to her.

"No you're not, so I'm apologizing for my behavior in Sky's pantry."

Their knees touched and she put out a hand to balance herself. "No need, Matt."

"I went too far. I misread you, Bridget. I'm sorry. I've been sorry since it happened."

Her face burned. "Don't apologize. I reacted badly. I was shocked, I guess."

"You had every right to be. It was stupid of me."

She stood up and dusted off her hands. "I was shocked at myself, not at you. Shocked that I reacted physically. I felt things I wasn't supposed to feel, feelings I thought were only for Todd. Until you kissed me, I thought I had all the answers and now I don't have any. *Shock*'s the perfect word. I'd been so hurt, so numb—then there you were kissing me, and I was stunned that I could have those kinds of feelings for someone I hardly knew, that I could be attracted—"

She stopped. "I think you know what I'm trying to say."

"I hope I do."

She smiled and in the dark he brushed her face. "I like what I'm hearing. Bridget, you've got your whole life ahead of you. There'll be lots of time for feelings that powerful."

She wanted to comment on his compassion and concern, but there was too much of a chance that he'd misconstrue her gratitude. Instead she repeated herself. "Thank you. Thank you for everything that weekend. I was dreading it and you made it bearable."

In response he smiled, maybe ruefully. "I'm glad I could help. You're a hell of a woman, Bridget."

"I didn't think I'd ever feel anything like that again." She trembled again. "What I'm saying terrifies me."

"Then stop talking." He leaned into the kiss as she stepped forward to meet him.

This time Matthew's touch was familiar as was the surge of desire it evoked in her. Apprehension was all she could muster in the way of self-defense.

He put his arms around her. "Will you kiss me now, Bridget?"

She nodded and in less time than it took for her heart to throb, he crushed his mouth against hers. He caressed her back, and under the wool of her sweater her nerves danced. She swayed against him, aching to be more intimate, yet holding back. It was enough to kiss him, to let the tantalizing exploration of his tongue match hers as they glided together and plunged, one then the other taking the lead.

Her fingers were open against his face. She felt his cheeks burn and when he turned and kissed the palms of her hands, she moaned. "Matthew."

"You sound breathless every time you say my name. It drives me wild, Bridget, even when you're angry."

"I'm not angry now."

"No, you're passionate, the way I've dreamed you'd be." He kissed her again and she moved into his embrace until the fit was as perfect as their first hug. Again he slid his hands over her shoulders and across her back. "You feel so good."

She swayed against him. "So do you."

"Too good. I don't have enough control to touch anything else."

"I would have stopped you if you had," she whispered at his ear. His muscles tightened and he moaned again as he returned to kissing her. He left her mouth and moved to the nape of her neck until she was nearly panting. A laugh bubbled up in her chest. She was happy.

"That was more of the reaction I was hoping for," he whispered.

"It's the reaction I've felt all along. That's why I was so upset, Matt."

"The unexpected can be damned exciting."

"Overwhelming and confusing."

"I suppose your sister would be appalled at me."

Bridget straightened up. "Make me a promise, Matthew. Promise me you'll keep Erin out of this."

He held her to his chest and spoke at her temple. "We discussed that in Sky's pantry."

"Then this is just between us."

"Yes, but tell me what 'this' is, Bridget."

"The revelation that I enjoy your company."

He chuckled. "Good start. Is there more?"

"You and me, moonlight, free time, country air."

"A break from reality? Pleasant diversion?"

Bridget smiled at him and relaxed. "All of the above."

Matt carelessly tossed a stick into the water. "If we're not careful, we'll have more than just Erin holding us under a microscope."

"Then let's be careful."

It was too dark to see his expression but she felt his look, his analysis of what she'd just implied. In reply, Matt draped his arm across her shoulder. When she'd snuggled up against him, they started back over the dike to the lawn.

"I suppose each of your brothers has seduced a woman or two out there under the stars."

Matt laughed softly. "My sisters-in-law have been exposed to more than their share of frost warnings."

"The spraying at night in the fall?"

"Spring, too, if necessary." As they climbed the porch steps, he glanced back over the darkened acres. "Can be damned romantic, I guess. I hardly think of myself as the seducing type."

"The most dangerous kind, Matthew."

He looked back at her.

"Oblivious," she added, as though in explanation. Erin was so right.

They went inside together and it wasn't until Bridget looked at Matt in the light of the kitchen that she saw the remnants of a flush. He kissed her chastely when they reached the top of the stairs, whispered, "Sleep well," and went into his own room.

Tuesday morning they all met again at the breakfast table. Erin was dressed for her administrative position at the Millbrook Medical Clinic in business maternity clothes. On the pretext of dressing for her day in the city, Bridget, too, was in a conservative skirt and simple blazer. She'd arranged her interview for ten-thirty and wanted only to be out from under the watchful eyes of her sister and the first and last of the Branigan brothers. Matthew had her head spinning. Hard as she tried, she couldn't make sense of her feelings.

Kevin served up cranberry juice and mushroom omelets while Bridget received last-minute instructions on driving into Boston. Erin recommended Copley Place and the Prudential area for shopping, which Bridget realized were within walking distance of her Newbury Street destination. The fates were with her.

Matthew was dressed for labor, as was Kevin, but he was headed for the boatyard, not the bogs. Well-worn jeans and a disreputable shirt did every bit as much for him as a suit jacket. Bridget looked at him surreptitiously and wondered what he would look like walking the hospital corridors in his white intern's coat. Devastating, she decided. Abruptly, she pushed her chair back and stood up.

Erin was the first to leave, followed by Kevin, who was off to a financial meeting with Holly and the company's CPA. It was Matt who walked her to her car.

"Don't do too much sightseeing. There's a lot I'd like to show you myself, if we can break away."

"You came to Millbrook to get away from Boston."

He shook his head. "I'm getting away from the work, not the sights. Showing you around might give me a new perspective on the same old stuff."

Bridget got into her car. "You've issued quite a few invitations already, Matt."

"Think about accepting a few of them," he replied as she started the engine.

Bridget reached the Back Bay section of Boston with little time to spare. Once she left the highway, the tangle of unfamiliar city streets forced her to concentrate on her driving, and once she found a parking lot with a free space, she was minutes from her appointment. She hurried up Newbury Street.

Did she want a job offer to come of this interview? Did she want Boston, after all? Matt had berated her for letting her feelings for Todd Harrison color her decisions. Was Matthew Branigan shading them, as well.

At Copley Square she glanced at Trinity Church before she searched the buildings for their numbers. She remembered the area from her college weekend at Erin's. Erin's and Matt's. Their Marlborough-street apartment was just two streets over and a few blocks down. As she reached her destination, she cleared her head. Business first.

Bridget O'Connor made a polished first impression, heightened by her confidence. Because no job was being offered and she wasn't at all sure she wanted a job—any job—in Boston, she wasn't nervous and had no qualms about putting her best foot forward.

Carla Benoit, a savvy woman of forty-three, made just enough small talk about Barrett to further put Bridget at ease and then explained the fund-raising and public-relations services the firm offered. "We work in-house, of course, creating campaigns and marketing strategy for clients—and we also consult. It's not unusual for us to provide assistance to a local firm, loan out a writer to an existing public-relations or fund-raising department for example."

After her own ten-minute descriptions, she asked Bridget specifically what she was looking for.

"On-the-job training. I know I can write and I feel that I have management skills. What I need is direction and guidance, a sort of editor to sharpen my work."

Carla looked again at the writing samples in Bridget's portfolio and shared examples of her own. The tour of the office included introductions to the small staff. Twenty minutes later they were shaking hands.

"It's been a pleasure," the older woman said. "You understand we don't have any immediate openings, but it's always worth the interview. I learned that a long time ago. This is an ever-changing business with clients popping up daily. Our focus and staff needs change with our client needs. That's why I wanted to see you, Bridget. How firm is your commitment to Atlanta?''

Bridget answered honestly. ''I have no job prospects down there yet, but I'm planning to drive down after Labor Day. I was hoping to come up with something by then. Leads, anyway.''

Carla turned to her files. ''We have contacts all over the country, of course. Would you like me to see if I can pull some information on Atlanta?''

''Would you?''

The older woman smiled. ''You give a very impressive interview, Bridget. If we can't use you, I'd be more than happy to make sure that somebody else knows what potential you have. Why don't I give you a call in the next day or two, if you'll leave your number in Millbrook. I'll see what I can come up with.''

Bridget hesitated. ''Would it be possible for me to call you? I'll be in and out and very hard to reach.''

''Of course, give me a little time to see what we have.''

''Thanks, very much.''

The sense of satisfaction Bridget drew from her interview carried her as she window-shopped on Newbury Street, poking her head into some of the more affordable shops. The possibility that Carla Benoit could use her influence to secure Bridget a job in Atlanta lifted the veil of indecision. Maybe something would develop during the week, something besides a smoldering relationship with Matthew Branigan.

She bought a linen blazer and a leather belt, and ate at the sidewalk table of Café Florian. On the pretext of walking off the calories, she headed across Back

Bay toward the Charles River. In less than five minutes, she was on Marlborough Street.

Bridget admired the nineteenth-century town houses as she walked, skirting an occasional pedestrian or broken sidewalk brick. This had been Erin's and Nancy Reed's block and it was still Matt's. She looked up at the fifth-floor windows. Matthew Branigan, her college fantasy, had sprung to life. As a matter of fact he was bursting with it.

Six

———

Bridget returned to Millbrook by midafternoon. A breeze had kicked up and the temperature was comfortable. She followed the sound of hammering and found Kevin and Matt in the house, working on the closet in the nursery.

"Lucky baby," she said at the door.

Matt wiped his brow with the back of his hand. "Welcome back. Traffic give you any trouble?"

"Not up and back. The city's a little confusing, though."

"Tradition has it that they just paved the old cow paths. Back Bay and the South End have the only logically laid out streets." He put the hammer down. "I'm glad you're back. Tide's right for an afternoon sail. We can have supper at the yacht club. What do you say?"

"Kevin doesn't need you?"

"Matt's on vacation, Bridget. I've had the better part of his day, already," Kevin replied.

"Just us?" When Kevin laughed, Bridget turned to him. "I meant because I don't know much about sailing. Maybe we should take some others along."

"You're all the crew I need, Bridget."

"Then I guess I accept."

"You sound reluctant."

"I have no idea what I'm in for."

Matt grinned. "Then you'll just have to trust me."

She did trust him, of course. She trusted him and enjoyed his company far more than she'd anticipated. The late afternoon was beautifully clear and the offshore breeze was stiffer in Plymouth than inland. They'd both changed into cotton slacks. Matt's polo shirt fit him perfectly, and Bridget wondered if he'd snuck as many glances at her boat-neck jersey.

"Perfect ingredients," Matt remarked from the parking lot of Saquish Yacht Club as they discussed the weather. "I hope you've got your sister's spunk."

"My sense of adventure used to get us all in trouble."

"What's life without a few risks?"

Bridget followed Matt through the clubhouse and out along the gangway. Boats of every description sat side-by-side in their individual slips, with hundreds more swaying in the bay on their moorings. Matt jumped lightly into the eighteen-foot catboat and turned to offer his hand. He held hers a trifle longer than necessary and the sensation of his touch lingered longer than she'd expected.

Matt unlocked the hatch cover, slid open the doors to the compact cabin and went below. He handed up the cockpit cushions, which Bridget arranged on the seats, and when she turned back to him he was grinning. Between thumb and forefinger he was holding up the top of a bikini.

"Recognize this?"

Bridget laughed as it swayed on its thin laces. "I've seen Megan in something like that. It's a little early in the season for bikinis."

Matt nodded. "No doubt she changed out of it the last time she was here because she was cold."

"What are you implying?"

He shrugged and came up from the cabin to sit next to her on the seat. "All any of us knew about Megan was that she was dead set against Erin marrying Kevin. I thought Jody was as happy in law as I am in medicine, and the next thing I know, he's in the midst of a career crisis and wants to be a cranberry grower. If he's fallen in love with an O'Connor on top of everything else, I wish him luck."

"Luck? Are we that formidable?"

He paused as if to choose his words. "Copperheaded, blue-eyed, determined hellions is what you are." He turned and tossed the bikini top back into the cabin.

Bridget scoffed. "Megan, Erin and I are as different from each other as you all are. You said so yourself at the wedding."

He put his head back against the coaming and stretched himself straight out, ankles crossed, face to the sun. He cupped his hands under the back of his head. "That may be, but you've got one thing in common."

He paused so long she thought he'd begun to doze. "Well?"

He opened one eye. "Every one of you sets Branigan blood to boiling."

"Do we now," she whispered as she got to her feet, ducked her head and went below into the cabin.

The small, efficient space was nothing more than padded berths on each side, a cooktop and toilet area. She picked up her sister's bathing suit top and stuck it in the next hammock slung at eye level to stow gear. The bikini bottom was already in it.

"Was I out of line?" Matt asked as he came into the cabin and stood in the galley area.

"Yes, I think so. I can't make sense of half the things you say. You imply one thing one minute and another the next."

"I'm a little confused myself."

"Then perhaps we'd better change the subject and get to the hoisting of the sail."

Matt nodded, gave her the kind of look she'd given him and stepped toward her. "Hand me that sailbag, please."

She nodded, but as she did Matt reached out. Gently, without the least pressure, he touched her face, and when she didn't object, he slid his hand into her hair. "It feels good to be alone with you, Bridget."

She nodded and took a step toward him, into his arms. As if he'd wanted only a sign of encouragement, he drew her sharply to him, crushing her in his arms. The boat swayed gently as a wake hit the stern and Bridget widened her stance to keep her balance. Her knees weakened the moment he kissed her and in unison they sank onto the berth.

"You and I have perfected the fine art of kissing," he whispered.

She moved until the length of her body lay within centimeters of his. "Do you intend to keep this to kissing?"

"Believe it or not, I brought you out here to sail."

"It seems foolish to start something we don't intend to finish."

He was quiet for a moment. "Are you frightened of finishing it?"

She rested her hand on his shoulder and felt the rapid rise and fall of his chest. "It isn't fear."

"You don't trust what you're feeling?" He covered her fingers and pressed until she felt the steady thunder under his ribs.

She laughed. "I know what I'm feeling physically. It's my emotions that have me so confused. It's happening too fast."

"The one thing we don't have is time, Bridget. You're moving south and all I've got left is the rest of this week. When my internship starts, I'm on a schedule that would exhaust a Clydesdale."

"So I've heard. Will it really be so bad?"

"I'll be on call every third day. It's possible to have to work seventy-two hours straight."

"Love of medicine will keep you going?"

"It better."

"Where will you practice once you finish your internship and residency?"

"First I have to decide *what* I'm going to practice, then I'll decide where I'll hang my shingle."

She sighed as the boat swayed under them and she kept her hand where he'd pressed it. "Your heart's pounding, all right."

"And yours?"

She looked into his eyes, so close and so full of passion. "You know what you do to mine."

Slowly, he put his hand in hers and leaned on his side. "Show me, Bridget."

"Matthew," she whispered.

He kissed her. "Nothing else. We won't, Bridget, we can't."

"I know," she whispered.

She kissed his fingertips and guided his hand to her waist. Her jersey was loose and the moment his hand grazed the skin of her stomach, every muscle in her contracted. He moved gently, up under the fabric, over her bare skin, rib by rib. He paused at the band of her bra and cradled her in his free arm.

She whispered his name again.

"You make it sound like music," he murmured. He kissed her softly as if to ensure that their passion stay in check. At the same time, he slid his hand beneath the strap of her bra and brushed it over her shoulder until her breast was free in his hand.

The sensation of Matt's touch sank into her. She knew he was holding back. She shared his desperation and fought for the same control, but as he moved his hand over her, it was a gesture of such languid and unconscious sensuality that she cried out and arched her back.

He groaned. "This is too dangerous. One more minute and I won't be able to stop."

She jammed her eyes shut. "One more minute and I won't want you to."

The pressure of his hand disappeared and Bridget opened her eyes to find Matt looking into them. He rolled away from her. Finally, he touched her hair. "Should I apologize?"

"No," she murmured, "don't ever apologize. Not for what you do or who you are." When she'd caught her breath, she rose from the bunk and went back up to the sunshine.

Matt followed and sat down next to her. "Are we smart to pull back or foolish?"

"Heaven only knows."

"Too soon?"

She sat down. "I honestly don't have an answer. Too complicated might be more accurate. Even more complicated than at the wedding. Now with Megan and Jody—"

"Could we leave them to their own predicaments?"

"While we create our own?"

Matt's eyes were dark. "Yes. I love my brothers, but I've been in the shadow of one or another of them all my life. If Jody's got the good sense to get himself involved with Megan, great. If their affair collapses, I'll be the first to offer sympathy. However, I don't want what might or might not happen between us this week to be influenced by them.''

''What might or might not happen could be influenced by any number of things, Doc.''

''I know that. I'm competing with memories of Todd, plans for Atlanta, sibling relationships—''

''You make my life seem awfully complicated.''

''What simplicity there is in either of our lives will last about another week. You know I'd like to take advantage of that.''

''What exactly are you proposing?''

He smiled and pulled the mainsail from the bag. ''Damned if I can put it in words, but I sure as hell recognize the feelings. Let's sail and see if we can figure it out.''

Under Matt's tutelage, Bridget was more of a help than she thought she would be. The single sail and wide, comfortable cockpit made the catboat easy to handle and responsive. Matt sat at the helm, changing sides with Bridget as they tacked in the open waters of Kingston and Duxbury bays. Between the scenery and the sailing, there was more than enough to keep both their minds occupied.

At dusk they motored back through the channel into the protected Plymouth waters behind the jetty. It was all boat talk until the sail was furled and *Respite* was again shipshape and secure for the night. However, the air was charged with suppressed emotion. Matt's cheeks glowed and his green eyes burned.

Bridget was heady with a sense of excitement, not risk or danger, just pure physical desire built from the ties that already bound them together. For the first time in her life, she was free from deadlines, from the demands of academia. She was free from the constraints of obligations and responsibility.

She watched Matt as she helped secure the boat. Desire welled up from some fathomless pool. He was part of what her sisters loved and part of what was new to her. She finally admitted to herself that he was still the college crush, the fantasy come to life—better in the flesh than anything she'd ever have conjured up on her own.

Thanks to Carla Benoit, she was more optimistic about employment in Atlanta, and the distance that would separate them shortly deepened her desire. Nothing could go wrong. A brief, intense affair with Matt Branigan would be cushioned by the safety net of her departure for Georgia. It dissolved the worry of family, the fishbowl of Millbrook. Soon he would be swallowed up by his work at the hospital and they would be separated by hundreds of miles. *Go for it,* a little voice urged her. *Take advantage of the respite from reality and let Matthew Branigan into your life.*

"Bridget?"

"I'm sorry, what did you say?"

"Go below and I'll hand down the cushions. Stow them the way they were, on either bunk."

She nodded, but Matt followed her into the cabin anyway. "Are you all right? You're flushed." Before she could reply, he pressed his index finger and thumb around her wrist.

"Matt, my pulse—"

"Just as I suspected."

"What do you suspect?"

He put his free hand back into her hair. "I suspect that you want me nearly as badly as I want you."

She put her open hands on his chest and then around his neck but they didn't kiss. It was too dangerous. The familiarity of his touch made her ache for more as they stood looking at each other.

"Could you handle this, Bridget, something brief, something that'll be over when we go back to our real lives?"

"Yes," she gasped. "You make me feel wonderful, Matt! Here and now is all I want."

"Now is all I can give you." He pulled her against the length of himself. "And what I need."

An invisible barrier dissolved. Bridget could feel the difference in herself as well as in Matt. The recognition and acceptance of what they were feeling freed her from the anxiety of fighting her own emotions. All she knew was that she was going to make love with this man.

They walked back along the docking slips, single file when necessary, which gave her a chance to savor his walk, the play of his muscles and the light on his shoulder. It thrilled her to know how it felt to be in his arms.

Matt suggested dinner in the informal dining room of the yacht club, and they sat amidst equally casual boat lovers. They found a corner table and over thick hamburgers and a glass of house wine he touched her hand. "You're quiet."

"Am I?" She gave him a studied look.

"There's a lot behind those blue eyes of yours."

"Frankly, I'm trying not to think too much about you. It ruins my digestion."

His smile was devilish. "What's your substitute?"

"I was thinking about what lies ahead for me."

"I do."

She laughed. "Besides you. I didn't go into Boston to shop this morning, Matt. I had a job interview. It was with Back Bay Associates, a fund-raising firm. They're an excellent group founded by two Barrett graduates, which is the only way I even got my foot in the door."

"Did they offer you something?" He looked surprised and his voice was hesitant.

"There wasn't much of a chance to begin with. That's why I didn't say anything. The surprise was that Carla Benoit, the president, has promised me some leads with her Atlanta connections. She couldn't have been more helpful."

"I think we'd all feel better knowing there was something waiting for you down there, if only interviews."

"You don't need to worry about me."

"*Worry*'s the wrong word. I'd like to see you do well."

"Live up to my potential?"

Now Matt grinned. "Am I sounding like your father?"

"Exactly."

Matt ate thoughtfully and when he glanced back at her, she was pensive. "I think about your father a lot, maybe because of the pressure he put on me when Erin moved in. He was so concerned about her during those first months on her own.''

"Erin, Megan and I are all levelheaded, Matt.''

"Neither you nor I were levelheaded a while ago, Bridget.''

"Are you sorry for what we've discussed?''

"Hugh would tell you to steer clear of casual affairs, I'm sure.''

"Yes. He always has.'' She glanced at Matt over her wineglass. "That's probably not what you wanted to hear. Stop feeling guilty just because you know my father. I'm a grown woman. I know what I'm doing.''

"You haven't done anything.''

"Not yet, but I haven't been able to concentrate on much of anything else in the past hour.''

He closed his eyes and sighed. "You'd better change the subject.''

Bridget watched his handsome face as he ate. There was such depth to his expression it was startling. "Is this the way it's always been for you and women, Matt? Has your schedule always come first?''

"There haven't been many, Bridget. I haven't had the time and medicine's made me well aware of the risks. I hope you're aware of them, too. I hope—'' He waved at the air and paused while color deepened his complexion.

Her own cheeks grew hot as she studied his clear, green gaze and waited.

Matt cleared his throat. "I hope when you're in Atlanta, you'll remember the risks, too. I hope you'll remember that you're Hugh O'Connor's daughter.''

"Matthew, what a sweet thing to say!''

He looked disconcerted. "I'm rarely accused of being sweet. I meant it, though. Your father's done a hell of a job."

"I'll tell him you said so."

Matt grinned. "I mentioned it to him at the wedding."

"Regarding Erin?"

"Regarding you, Bridget. You've got a wonderful life ahead of you. Hugh was damned worried about you in April, but you're a different person from the one I escorted at the wedding. It's as if you've come back to life."

"Getting over Todd hasn't been easy."

"It takes time, Bridget."

"Time and some pleasant diversions, Doc."

Matt leaned over and kissed her. "Let's go home and find some privacy."

Bridget looked at the tourist bustle as Matt drove through the Plymouth streets. After inching their way along the waterfront, past the *Mayflower II* and Plymouth Rock, Matt turned up a sharp hill.

"Shortcut?"

He nodded. "Goes past Jody's too. I'll point it out. There's somebody else who could use some pleasant diversion," he said as they spotted the attorney Branigan halfway up Saquish Street, getting out of his car.

Jody's vibrancy, so evident at the wedding, had been replaced with obvious fatigue. Matt idled the car just long enough to make small talk.

"Get some sleep, bro. Doctor's orders."

"Can't say lack of sleep's the problem, Matt."

"Then figure out what's got you so strung out and face it."

Jody saluted and looked through the car to Bridget. "I'm used to an earful from my older brothers. The youngest graduates from medical school and now I have to listen to him, too."

Bridget leaned over Matt and looked up at Jody. "Listen to your own heart. There's no other way."

He smiled ruefully. "Are you sure you're related to Megan?"

"Excuse me?"

He waved off the remark. "Never mind. Finish your ride. Say hello to everybody at the bogs and don't let Matt bore you to death with medical talk."

Bridget laughed. "Matt could never bore me to death."

Dusk settled into darkness as they drove the quiet back roads. "I'm worried about him."

"I can see that," Bridget replied.

Jody, his current circumstances, his personality and his relationship with Megan kept the conversation focused until they were back at the bogs. When they turned onto the long Branigan drive, Matt's headlights caught Erin and Kevin as they walked up the hill.

"Any interest in a childbirth video?" Kevin asked as he came to the car. "Erin's going to give Holly and Drew a refresher course."

Matt laughed. "I'm on a vacation from medicine. You guys enjoy it. Pay attention, Kevin, you'll need it, too, in a couple of months."

Kevin laughed and glanced at his watch. "We'll be back by eight-thirty. There's strawberry shortcake in the fridge if you didn't fill up at the yacht club."

Matt thanked him and continued down the hill. "Erin's lucky to have such a supportive family around her," Bridget murmured.

"We're lucky to have Erin."

They got out of the car together and Matt took her hands in his. "I don't want to talk about Erin or Megan or Jody or any other damned thing."

"Could this have anything to do with the fact that we're alone till eight-thirty?"

"Everything."

"Matthew."

He caressed her shoulder. "Whenever you're at a loss for words, you whisper my name."

"I like saying it."

"I like hearing it."

They walked through the damp grass toward the house and Matt fell silent. For Bridget, the night sounds around them were amplified by the pulse pounding in her ears. Peepers, a distant bark, the soft *whoosh* of the breeze in the pine tops played in her head while her heart danced. The sound of their matched footsteps on the porch thundered. Matt paused at the door and looked at her in the shadows, deepened by the contrast of the porch light. What Bridget saw in his expression changed the rhythm of the dance to a hard, fast pounding.

"You feel it, too," he said.

"It was quite an afternoon."

He cupped her face. His hands were cool against her flaming skin as he nuzzled her neck. "You're burning up."

"Memory is a powerful thing," she whispered.

"So is anticipation." He kissed her face in a dozen places. "You taste the way you did this afternoon, like sea spray," he murmured.

"I need a shower."

"Not yet."

She kissed his jaw and ran her tongue along the hollow of his throat. "Salt water," she whispered.

He groaned and the gentle pressure of his open fingers tightened. With one hand he held the back of her head and with the other he widened at the base of her spine.

His name caught in her throat as she pressed against him. Every nerve in her body hummed with the memory of how she'd felt in his arms. She could have made love with him there, standing in the June night on the Branigan porch.

"Bridget," he moaned. "I can't play. I can't touch you like this without wanting all of you, not after this afternoon." He pushed her to arm's length. "Will you come upstairs with me?"

In reply she opened the screen door and waited for him to follow.

"Your room," he said as they reached the top of the stairs. "The way I feel right now, any room would do. I nearly made love with you on that narrow bunk in the boat."

They went into the room together. It was dusky, full of shadows thrown by the contrast of the outside floodlights spilling through the open window. One shaft fell cleanly across the four poster bed. "It's beautiful in this light," she whispered.

"So are you. Keep it this way. It was meant for making love."

Bridget sank onto the mattress. "Have you made love here, Matt?"

"Never. Not on the boat, either."

"I'm your first?"

"You're my first, Bridget."

He closed the door and came and sat beside her on the bed, suddenly awkward.

"Where shall we start?" she managed.

"Exactly where we left off."

She fell back and he followed, sliding his arm under her, moving her in next to him, closer than they'd been on the bunk, if that were possible. Again he slid his free hand tantalizingly under her jersey, over her ribs to the thin fabric of her bra, kissing her this time as he moved. "I was right here."

The warmth of his fingers burned her skin. She'd dreamed of this moment, fought it, talked about it, analyzed it to death. Yet nothing prepared her for the rush of desire that swept her as he fingered the strap of her bra this second time. Underneath the jersey he moved his hand inside the cup. Slowly he grazed her flesh with his knuckles. She looked into his face, wide-eyed.

He was watching her, then suddenly, he closed his eyes and groaned. "So soft," he whispered as he cupped her other breast. Rhythmically he repeated the movements, back and forth with his fingers against the tender weight of her flesh. Back and forth. He began to move his body in time to it. She rocked, as well.

She moaned into his kiss and welcomed the plunder of his tongue, stunned at the sensations he incited. ''Matthew,'' she whispered.

He groaned immediately. ''Say it again.''

She murmured his name over and over in the same rhythm and he did nothing to hide the desire it built in him.

Underneath the jersey, her skin ignited. When he finally stopped, it was to kneel and free her from the shirt and bra. He hovered over her and kissed her mouth until she drove her hands into his hair and brought him back down to her.

''Bridget...the moonlight,'' he groaned. His breath tickled her throat and when he used his tongue to leave a trail back to her breasts, she cried out. He nuzzled the soft flesh, then kissed the perimeter of each nipple leaving them moist and suddenly cold in the night air. She gasped and arched, aching for the heat.

He repeated it quickly and she arched again. The rhythm built until she was mindless with the sensation. When he raised his head to look at her, she cradled his face and kissed him, then slid her hands over his shoulders. His breathing was labored as she pulled his shirt from his jeans. She lifted the cotton over his head and slid her open hands over his chest. She rocked beneath him again, caressing his back, up to his shoulders and down to the base of his spine. His bare skin was hot, and she kissed his chest, whispering his name with what little breath she had as she left her own trail.

Her hands fell to his waistband and he matched her with rough, urgent movements until the rest of their clothes were piled on the floor.

He reached for his pants, for the protection they needed, and she fell back into the pillows again, bringing him with her. When she relaxed under him, he straddled her hips and kissed her with a new urgency. He caressed her intimately, hungrily this time, no longer waiting for her reaction. The rough friction of her hands on his skin, the shock of his kisses on her breasts had worked their magic. Nothing she'd ever fantasized about him had prepared her for the open, aching need yawning in her.

Their rhythm increased. As she drove her hands along his hips and down his thighs he caressed her until it was impossible to tell one set of cries from the other. He held her still and she was aware only of the power of the moment. "Now, Bridget," he groaned. She welcomed him as he settled over her.

Matt's rhythm guided them as she clung to him and savored his hunger for her. She moved with him as he controlled their journey but the ache deepened, piercing her from heart to hips. She was suddenly torn by the desire for release and the need to hold the moment. She couldn't think and no longer felt anything but the widening torment. "Matthew!"

He held her tighter, until she felt his heart pounding savagely against hers. Reality fell away as his urgency became hers; his need became hers. He reacted immediately as if he felt what she felt. Once more she cried out, and this time ecstasy engulfed her.

Seven

Bridget's sudden release was matched by Matt's, and they clung to each other, holding the moment as if they could suspend time. He kissed her tenderly and simply whispered her name.

They lay together, satiated. She longed for the luxury of curling up in Matthew's arms and falling asleep, but time had run out. Kevin and Erin were due back. With a final kiss, she got up and left the room. She heard her sister's voice as she turned on the shower.

As she lathered, she expected to feel resentment, but she realized that Erin's and Kevin's presence was what would keep what was developing between her and Matt under control. Without the family chaperons there was far too much chance that three more days and nights in his arms would cement an intimacy—at least on her part—that she wouldn't be able to put behind herself. Todd Harrison had burned her badly. Kevin and Erin were just the interruption she needed to keep her feet firmly planted on the ground, no matter where her heart was for the moment.

When she'd dressed, she followed the voices to the kitchen and found Matt, fresh from his own shower, deep in a sailing discussion with his brother and sister-in-law while they dished out strawberries.

Bridget picked up the plastic video case from the counter. "How was your film?"

"Excellent. It's a new one from the clinic I had to screen. Since Ryan and Sean delivered Maria at home during that storm, I thought Drew and Holly might like to take a look at a hospital situation."

"When is she due?"

"Four weeks." Erin patted her stomach and looked at Kevin.

Matt leaned over and touched Erin's arm. "I've got my stethoscope in the car. Want to listen to the baby's heartbeat?"

"Great idea! Maybe Kevin can figure out who's in there."

For no reason she was willing to name, emotion tightened Bridget's throat as she watched Matt minister to her sister after he'd returned. Erin shifted in the kitchen chair and discreetly shifted her cotton top.

Matt knelt on the oak floor, listened and shook his head. "Give me a minute. This isn't nearly as sophisticated as an ultrasound monitor." His sudden grin brought a change in Kevin's expression as well, but Matt held him off as he cocked his head. "Hold on...there...wait...." He pressed the earpieces and it wasn't until he pulled them off and said, "Your turn," to Kevin that anyone took a breath.

When they'd all listened, Matt stood up and patted Erin's knees. "When's your next appointment?"

"I'm scheduled for an ultrasound on Wednesday."

"Good. You'll hear it a lot more clearly in your OB's office. You'll see it, too."

"Any names yet?" Bridget asked.

"Nothing we can agree on."

While Kevin cleared the table, Max and Domino, the retrievers, sauntered in from the next room. Matt picked up his stethoscope and issued an invitation to Bridget. "Beautiful moon for walking dogs under."

Erin and Kevin said good-night and Bridget followed Matt down the steps of the porch, into the moonlight. "It's hard to believe that the first time I saw you walk across this lawn I didn't know which brother you were."

"I'd have known you anywhere," he replied. "You're pure O'Connor, but unique."

"Not a carbon copy of Erin or Megan?"

He pulled her into his chest and kissed her tenderly. "No, Bridget, you're absolutely priceless." He paused and added "Last April I'd never have guessed we'd share anything beyond the wedding." He turned to look out over the darkened bogs. "I don't want anyone hurt by this."

"Then be glad Kevin and Erin are here."

Matt nodded. "Chaperons? I am, and in a way I'm glad you have Atlanta to look forward to."

"Because next week you disappear into the bowels of New England Regional Hospital never to be seen again?"

"Truer than you know."

"I hope you'll come up for air, occasionally."

He touched her face. "You'd deserve better."

"Guilt? I thought we'd been through all that."

"We have."

"Then enjoy the moment, Matthew. I am."

He put the stethoscope to her breastbone and when she'd given him time to listen, she moved it to his own heart. Matt put the earpieces in her ears. "Beat for beat, they're pretty evenly matched," she said.

When he'd put the instrument away, they started off along the cart path, dogs ahead, night air sweet. "Any twins in your family?"

"As a matter of fact, My Grandmother Flynn always said her mother was a triplet, but the only one who survived childhood. There's no record in our family Bible, though, so I don't know if it—" She stopped on the dike. "Why do you ask?"

He shrugged. "I thought I might have heard a second heartbeat."

"Two? Why didn't you say something?"

"It's only a stethoscope. If there's something significant there, her obstetrician will pick it up on the fetal heart monitor soon."

"Twins!"

"Don't say anything, Bridget. I'm not an obstetrician."

"No, but there are multiple births in both our families."

"Jamie and Kate Branigan only produced male siblings and those six have only produced female children. Don't second-guess genetics, Bridget."

She put her arm through his. "Only two of your brothers have children, so far, Matt. Anything can happen."

"That much is true."

"You love medicine, don't you."

"Yes."

"You'll be a wonderful doctor, Matt. It shows in your face every time you minister to someone. It's a gift. Erin's always said so, and I can see how right she is."

"That means a lot."

"It's true." She looked at the distant lights in Drew's house on the hill as they turned back toward the homestead. "Are you sorry you missed Holly's home delivery?"

"Very, but it was tough enough for Holly with Ryan and Sean meeting the emergency. It's just as well that I was in school."

"They managed without you."

"Babies are born when they're good and ready. My brothers are emergency medical technicians and they had Holly's OB on the phone. Minimal risk. It would have been a lot chancier trying to drive to the hospital."

"What a family night that must have been!" She snuggled into his side as he slung his arm over her shoulder.

"Family is what makes life worth living, even with its problems."

Silhouette's

Best Ever "Get Acquainted" Offer

Look what we'd give to hear from you

6 FREE GIFTS 6

Return This Sticker
and Get 6 Gifts—FREE
Compliments of Silhouette

▲ GET ALL YOU ARE
ENTITLED TO—AFFIX STICKER
TO RETURN CARD—MAIL TODAY ▲

This is our most fabulous offer ever . . .
AND THERE'S STILL MORE INSIDE.
Let's get acquainted.
Let's become friends—

Look what we've got for you:

... A FREE 20k gold electroplate chain
... plus a sampler set of 4 terrific Silhouette Desire® novels, specially selected by our editors.

... PLUS a surprise mystery gift that will delight you.

All this just for trying our Reader Service!

If you wish to continue in the Reader Service, you'll get 6 new Silhouette Desire® novels every month—before they're available in stores. That's SNEAK PREVIEWS for just $2.24* per book— 26¢ less than the cover price—plus only 69¢ postage and handling for the entire shipment!

Plus There's More!

With your monthly book shipments, you'll also get our newsletter, packed with news of your favourite authors and upcoming books—FREE! And as a valued reader, we'll be sending you additional free gifts from time to time—as a token of our appreciation for being a home subscriber.

THERE IS NO CATCH. You're not required to buy a single book, ever. You may cancel Reader Service privileges anytime, if you want. All you have to do is write "cancel" on your statement or simply return your shipment of books to us at our cost. The free gifts are yours anyway. It's a super-sweet deal if ever there was one. Try us and see!

Get 4 FREE full-length Silhouette Desire® novels.

Plus

this lovely 20k gold electroplate chain

Plus

a surprise free gift

▼ PLUS LOTS MORE! MAIL THIS CARD TODAY ▼

Silhouette's Best-Ever "Get Acquainted" Offer

Yes, I'll try Silhouette books under the terms outlined on the opposite page. Send me 4 free Silhouette Desire® novels, a free electroplated gold chain and a free mystery gift.

326 CIS 8155 (C-S-D-03/90)

PLACE STICKER FOR 6 FREE GIFTS HERE

NAME _____

ADDRESS _____ APT. _____

CITY _____

PROV. _____ POSTAL CODE _____

Don't forget...

... Return this card today and receive 4 free books, free electroplated gold chain and free mystery gift.

... You will receive books before they're available in stores.

... No obligation to buy. You can cancel at any time by writing "cancel" on your statement or returning
a shipment to us at our cost.

If offer card is missing, write to: Silhouette Books®
P.O. Box 609, Fort Erie, Ontario L2A 5X3

**Business
Reply Mail**

No Postage Stamp
Necessary if Mailed
in Canada

Postage will be paid by

Silhouette® Books
P.O. Box 609
Fort Erie, Ontario
L2A 9Z9

Canada Post
Postes Canada
125

"No matter how much distance you put between them."

"Like the length of the East Coast?"

"Physical distance or emotional, Matthew."

Bridget went to her room satisfied with the way things were. She'd taken what Matt could offer her and the fact that it was all for the moment suited her fine. Professional promises lay on the horizon. She fell asleep thinking, not about her own circumstances, but Erin's. Twins!

Friday dawned clear and warm and the second floor was quiet by the time Bridget woke. She dressed for work in the garden and went downstairs to find the four older Branigan men drinking coffee. Financial statements and technical papers on pest control were laid out in front of them. They greeted her as she came into the room. She helped herself to breakfast and took juice and cereal around the partition into the family room.

Matt was on the couch, putting the phone back in its cradle. "Good morning. You're awfully flushed. Feeling all right?"

"That much maleness is disconcerting this early in the morning!"

Matt smiled. "There was a time when they prided themselves on drawing that reaction from innocents like you. You should have seen them when Holly tried to outmaneuver us."

"She locked horns with an ornery bunch of bachelors."

"That she did."

Bridget ate as she relaxed. "Jody's the only one missing."

"I was up all night thinking about him. I've talked him into taking the day off."

"Good idea."

"More than the day, actually. We're going to take the boat overnight. Try to sail out to Provincetown and back."

"In the hopes you can get to the bottom of what's eating at him?"

"I know what's eating at him—he's leaving environmental law and coming back home to work."

"A decision that big needs a sounding board. Somebody not connected to a cranberry bog."

"That's exactly what I told him. I'm sorry—"

She put up her hand. "Matthew, I have no strings on you. This is your vacation and your family. The separation might do us some good, too."

He knit his brow. "I'm going back to Boston Sunday. I figured that would cool things soon enough."

She leaned against his shoulder and whispered, "This way Monday morning won't be such a shock to our overheated systems."

"I wish to hell I could take you with us."

"It defeats the purpose. Jody needs time with you, man-to-man, brother-to-brother. No women."

"While I'm gone, you might have a word or two with a member of your own family."

"Meaning Megan's part of his problem?"

"According to Kevin, yes." He swallowed the last of some juice.

"When did you and Kevin talk?"

"This morning."

She tried to sound blasé as she listened to the male voices in the next room. "I suppose he's got an opinion about us, as well."

"It's his role in life. Kevin has an opinion on everything, mostly Megan, at the moment. Talk to her for me."

"I'll try."

On the pretext of free time and an interest in a tour of the radio station, Bridget arranged to see her sister that morning and added lunch as a thank-you.

"Lovely view of the harbor," Bridget commented as the waitress set salads in front of them. "Did you know Jody and Matt have left for Provincetown?"

"No. I haven't spoken with Jody recently."

"Little time away for both of them. *Respite*'s an appropriate name for the boat, don't you think?"

"I'm sure Matt can use the vacation, if that's what you're hinting at."

"Matt and I sailed across the bay yesterday. I understand you and Jody have taken *Respite* out a few times, too." Bridget watched Megan poke at her salad.

"Yes, I've been on the boat."

"I thought so. I found your bikini in the hammock."

"Did you."

"Are you in love with him?"

"Could I please eat my shrimp in peace?"

"That means yes."

"That means mind your own business, little sister. Jody and I have nothing in common. We got carried away—that's no secret, but no, I'm not in love with him."

"Matt and I saw Jody yesterday. He's not the same man I met in April."

Megan sighed and nibbled on a bite of lettuce.

"He shows all the signs of a man miserably in love," Bridget added.

"Honestly, how would you know? Your fling with Todd Harrison doesn't make you an expert."

"It doesn't take an expert to spot the symptoms. Don't you see that he's in love with you?"

"He has his own life to straighten out. Love should be the furthest thing from his mind. When he *does* settle down, I hope he finds some cheerful nature lover accustomed to hard work, agriculture and country life."

"He has."

"I mean somebody who likes it!" she said with a glare. "All right, Jody and I were involved. I was foolish to get so wrapped up in him, but it's over. All the things that we held in common have vanished. It would be foolish to go on. You might as well know that I've put in a request for a transfer."

"From WJQG? Megan, they just sent you here to the Plymouth station!"

"Transfers happen all the time. We have an affiliate in Baltimore."

"Be serious!"

"I've never been more serious in my life."

"Running away never solved anything."

"And you're not? Atlanta isn't an escape from Todd?"

Bridget sighed. "I'm over Todd. Matt's made me see that." She flinched under her sister's scrutiny.

"You and Matt? This must have the rest of them howling." Megan shook her head.

"Don't jump to conclusions, Megs. We've gotten to be close friends this week."

"How close? You haven't—"

"No, we haven't," Bridged fibbed. "He's a wonderful person, that's all. He'll make a wonderful doctor."

"If he doesn't decide he'd rather be a wonderful cranberry grower."

"Bitterness was never your style, Megan."

"I'm entitled to my opinions. I'm glad you're all set for Atlanta. It'll save a lot of heartache. Leave the Branigans to Erin."

Bridget smiled. "Do you think they argue as much as the O'Connors?"

"I'm tired of thinking about what Branigans do and don't do. Jody's made a monumental change in his life, one that he thinks will make him happy. I'm sure he's got a tough row to hoe ahead of him and I wish him well, Bridget." Her voice shook. "It's his life, not mine. Now could we please change the subject before I ruin my mascara?"

By three o'clock Bridget had returned to the bogs and cultivated nearly every row in Kevin's vegetable garden. She wiped her brow, set the scarecrow back amid the potato hills and tried to dismiss thoughts of Megan and Jody. She also tried to dismiss thoughts of Matthew and the fact that she'd lied to her sister about the depth of the relationship. Love was all she'd thought about as she'd worked: fraternal love, physical love, emotional love, spiritual love. She'd pulled weeds and assured herself that she didn't feel anything but maybe the first for Matthew Branigan. The deception made her as light-headed as did the heat.

When she'd finished in the garden, she wandered across the lawn and up the hill to Drew and Holly's. All the men she'd met in the kitchen that morning were on the small, six-acre patch of Bittersweet Bogs, separated from the Greek Revival house by an orchard. Bridget sat down and leaned back against the trunk of an apple tree to watch them. She saw bits of Matt in each of his brothers. His hair was identical to Drew's in color, his eyes most like Sean's. Kevin had the same way of moving his shoulders and Ryan's build was a close match. She was relieved that Matt wasn't among them. To further clear her mind, Bridget got up and started down the hill toward Kevin and Erin's. It was time to call Back Bay Associates and get the names of the business contacts in Atlanta.

Bridget grabbed her portfolio and had paper and pencil ready to take down whatever Carla might have come up with. She tapped out the number and prepared for a pleasant and productive conversation. Twenty minutes later a stunned Bridget O'Connor hung up the phone. Sky Branigan appeared in the family room, looking for Ryan. Bridget waved meekly as she crossed the room.

Sky looked puzzled. "Are you all right? You're awfully pale."

"Unexpected news. Back Bay Associates has taken on two new national accounts. They've offered me a job in Boston."

"Fabulous!"

Bridget sighed. She wasn't at all sure how she felt about the offer—or the ramifications. She hadn't even digested the news. However, before she could explain any of that to Sky, the sound of heavy steps on the farmer's porch made her stop. Kevin and his brothers had returned and were stepping aside for Erin as she, too, made her way into the house.

It was Sky who innocently announced the fact that Bridget had wonderful news, and they all waited expectantly for her to explain it.

Eight

—

It's not what I'd planned," Bridget protested long after dinner when the subject was broached over the last of the strawberries.

Sky and Ryan had stayed to eat, and Bridget had managed successfully to steer clear of the subject until then.

"Atlanta was an escape, and you know it. You're certainly over Todd now," Erin said.

"It makes no sense whatever to go all the way down there with nothing waiting when a plum like this is already in your lap, Bridget," Kevin said.

"The starting salary's too low for me to rent anything on my own. None of my close friends—"

"My house!"

Bridget stopped and looked at Sky.

"The Beacon Hill house is empty. You'd be the perfect tenant. You'd be doing us a favor, honestly. No one in the family's using it. Ryan and I are lucky if we're up there once a month."

"From what I know of your family house, I'd be lost in it. Probably scared to death, too."

"It has a full alarm system and it's in a safe area."

"I meant scared of all those priceless antiques!"

Sky waved aside her doubts. "At least use it while you look for an apartment."

Ryan grinned. "You'll never get a better offer. Sunday, Matt has to go back to Marlborough Street. Why don't we all go into Boston and have dinner at the house. You can look it over."

"I don't know."

Kevin looked at his wife. "You haven't suggested that she stay with Matthew."

Erin laughed. "Too overprotective. Matt would probably set a curfew and rearrange the jaw of the first man who kept her out too late."

Bridget flushed but held back her protest. The less said the better. The conversation continued, and she watched and listened, feeling more like an eavesdropper than a participant. Down to the last family member, somebody had an opinion about her future and seemed perfectly willing to take on responsibility for seeing it through. Before the end of the evening she'd been swept up in half a dozen ideas by more than that many Branigans. Erin was the most enthusiastic Branigan of all.

For the first time, Bridget thought about the pressure that kind of concern had put the brothers under.

No wonder so many of them had rebelled. By the time Bridget went up to bed, the next year of her life had been mapped out in minute detail. She felt ambivalent, at best.

Saturday morning Bridget played tennis with Sky at the Millbrook Country Club and returned after lunch to nearly deserted bogs. The family had scattered, including Erin, who'd left a note saying she was at Megan's. The thought of added advice from her middle sister was enough to drive Bridget over the cart path on a solitary walk. *Solitary*, she decided, was a word with which a few Branigans were familiar.

She was thinning the last of the spinach crop when Matt returned from his sail. He pulled down the rutted drive and into the courtyard next to the garden. Her heart jumped at the sight of him. He was windblown. The fresh air and physical demands of his trip had added erotism to the impression he made as he walked toward her. Desire was in his eyes. The closer he got the more he smiled and the faster her heart pounded. He came inside the fencing and swung her around in his arms.

"Matt!"

"God, I missed you." He nuzzled her neck and gave her a salty kiss. "Great sail, gorgeous weather."

She held him longer than necessary, molding herself to his thighs and chest. His physical response was immediate. "I wanted you there with us. I wanted *you*, for that matter."

"I can tell."

"I don't suppose we're alone."

"I'm not sure your family knows the meaning of the word." She stepped back reluctantly and brushed his hair with her fingers. "How's Jody?"

"You're changing the subject."

"No choice," she muttered.

He took a slow breath. "I suppose you're right. Jody's fine. I've never known a woman to get him down. If Megan's calling it quits, so be it. He's calling the shots on this one. He's leaving his law practice and there's no turning back."

"You agree with him?"

"I agree he's got to live his own life."

"That's not easy to do in your family."

"Meaning?"

She shook out a head of spinach and put it in the basket at her feet. "Meaning you all tend to live one another's lives. It can be exhausting."

Matt looked at her basket. "Since you won't let me make mad, passionate love with you here on the spinach beds and I'm overdue for a shower, I might as well give you a hand. Could I talk you into going out to dinner tonight? It's my last night of freedom."

Last night. "Someplace on the water?"

"Suits me. It'll be a long while till I see it again."

"Brutal schedule starting Monday."

"Brutal."

They worked side-by-side while Matt entertained her with stories of the sailing trip and explanations of the grueling life of a medical intern in a Harvard teaching hospital. He made it clear that the Matthew Branigan she'd glimpsed all week was about to disappear from sight.

* * *

They ate at a waterfront café near the yacht club. Through dinner Matt elaborated on his trip with Jody, and when the subject inevitably turned to medicine, he described the rotation system from emergency-ward duty to intensive care and surgery that awaited him. Throughout the meal he was subdued, which she assumed was due to the rigors ahead.

"Are you all right?" she asked at the end.

"Certainly." He busied himself with the check. She folded and refolded her napkin. When he looked at her napkin, his green eyes were dark.

His mood darkened during the ride home, and he was nearly withdrawn by the time they reached the bogs.

When they got out of the car, she stayed on the driveway. The air was still warm and smelled of early summer. "You're not yourself tonight. All the way home I've been trying to decide whether it's Jody or what you're facing Monday morning."

Matt turned so they were both caught in the floodlight. "It's you, Bridget."

She paled at his frankness.

"We've been together for hours—in the garden, at the house, through an entire meal. I've given you every chance. Why the hell did I have to hear from Kevin that you took a job in Boston?"

She flushed.

"It's monumental news," he continued. "A complete about-face, and all evening I've been thinking any minute you'll bring up the subject. Nothing! You haven't said a single word about it."

Her flush deepened. "I would have told you."

"When? Tomorrow when we all go to Beacon Hill? Some afternoon when I run into you in Copley Square?"

"I don't want to live on Beacon Hill. Since the wedding you've known that I don't want Erin running my life. It's worse now—I've got every Branigan in Millbrook giving me advice. I haven't had time to sort out my feelings. I've hardly digested the news myself."

"They're just trying to help. You should be damned appreciative you've got all these connections."

"As if I couldn't have done any of it on my own merit?"

"That's not what I meant."

"Well that's how it sounded. Just be glad I didn't turn them down."

"You'd have been a fool to have even considered it."

"Matt!"

"Have you given Todd Harrison so much as a thought this week?"

"You know I haven't."

"Your Atlanta motive is gone. Boston makes much more sense." He studied her solemn expression. "You don't look convinced."

"There are other things to consider."

"Branigan and O'Connor meddling."

"Yes."

Matt looked out at the bogs. "And us," he said to the view.

"Maybe. You and I started something this week we knew would be finished by tomorrow. You're off to your internship and I was to be off, too, far out of reach. It would have been perfect the way it was."

"But?"

"I was afraid you'd think I took the job because of you."

He hesitated and finally replied, "A ridiculous notion, of course."

"Yes."

"Accepting the offer because of me makes as much sense as not taking a job because of Todd."

"I'm glad you see it that way."

"Nothing's changed, Bridget. We still have to cool things off tomorrow, whether you're working in Boston or not. My schedule will take care of that."

"Good," she managed. "We'll both be busy. That's the way I want it."

"That's the way it has to be."

They went into the house. Jody, Sky and Ryan were in the living room with Kevin and Erin, and any further conversation became impossible. Matt made small talk about their dinner and Bridget chattered about her job offer, then left them all, including Matthew. Once upstairs, however, her restlessness increased. Matthew Branigan agitated her as no one else ever had.

She pulled a sweater over the shirtwaist dress she'd worn to dinner and went back downstairs, announcing that she was going for a walk.

Kevin nodded at his younger brother. "Make sure she doesn't fall in a bog."

She should have protested. She should have insisted on strolling alone. She should have quelled her racing pulse. Instead she waited until Matthew went upstairs for a fleece pullover and left with him.

"Moon's nearly full," he said when they were out in the lawn.

"Bright enough to see by. You can go back."

"You don't need me."

"I know the way."

"Then let me show you another."

Instead of taking the cart path out to the dike, Matt started off in the direction of the orchard bordering the smaller patch of Holly's Bittersweet Bogs.

In the moonlight the neat rows of semidwarf apple trees cast undulating shadows. "MacIntosh," Matt said. "We all planted them with Peter right after my parents died."

"You didn't have your parents very long, did you?"

"I was five when they died. It made for an interesting childhood."

"I'm sorry," she said again.

"I didn't mean it sarcastically. So far it's been a wonderful life." He looked at her in the silvery light until she glanced up at him. "Full of surprises," he whispered as he touched her face.

Bridget put her hand over his and sighed. "Why did you walk me over here?"

"Why did you follow?"

They answered each other by moving under a drooping branch and when he kissed her, Bridget's restlessness deepened into a well-defined ache. "Because our lives will change on Monday and this is all we have left."

Matt held her tighter as if he'd longed for that reply. "I've hated the thought of not holding you again. Now that I know how it feels when you touch me, what you can do." He put his fingers on her cheek as her flush returned. "Once more, Bridget, for both of us."

"Here?"

He pulled back her sweater and caressed the fabric covering her breasts. "I've wanted to make love with you since I got back from the sail. I've been ready since I felt that readiness in you, back in the garden this afternoon."

"Maybe that's why I didn't tell you about the job. I couldn't bear the thought of anything changing until it had to."

"It doesn't have to yet. We still have tonight."

"Just this little part of it."

"Then we'll make it a part to remember." Roughly he worked the top buttons through their holes on the front of her dress.

"Under the moon and apple blossoms," she gasped as she slid his belt through its buckle.

"God, yes." He moaned against her mouth as she welcomed him there. He plunged and traced the tender inside of her lips at the moment her dress fell open for him. The shock of the cold night air was replaced by the heat of his hand.

"I won't undress you. It's too cold. Just enough." He teased the flesh under her bra until her nipples were rock hard. "Just enough." Pleasure coursed through her and she shuddered against him.

"I've been ready—" His words died as he responded, pressing back and back again. He left just enough space between them for her to finish her journey at his waistband and for him to finish his.

"Hurry," one of them said or maybe it was both. Matt stepped from his clothes and she sank with him to the grass. As he whispered over and over how good she felt, he caressed everything he'd exposed under her dress. Bridget's cries were as soft as the wind but she stoked his desire with strokes as rough as his.

She couldn't tell whether it was her touch or the feel of her under his own hands that pushed Matt over the edge. It didn't matter. They were locked and lost in the delicious conundrum of wanting it to go on forever and needing the ecstasy of release.

Bridget hovered with Matt on the edge of endurance, thin as a knife blade. She wanted to be a sounding board for his pleasure this last time, and she pressed his hips as he plunged. Ecstasy gripped him and became the source of hers. They rocked together in an intimate rhythm completely private, now familiar and all theirs.

Finally, when it was too cold and damp to stay any longer, they reluctantly got to their feet and made themselves presentable. On the way back, Bridget told him what Carla Benoit had described to her. She would be starting as a fund-raising copywriter, learning on the job from some of the best minds in the business. In their own ways, Bridget and Matt were already stepping back from the passion that had drawn them together so carelessly.

When they'd reached the edge of the lawn, Matt caressed her shoulder. "Has this week been a mistake?"

"Because we've made love?"

"Yes."

She sighed. "I don't want to think so."

"But you don't want it to get in the way, either."

"Matt, you'd made it very clear that it can't go on."

"Bridget, I— We could work things out."

The tone of his voice made her wince. "Because I won't be hundreds of miles away any longer? Guilt never did anyone any good. A clean break and a nice friendship would mean a whole lot more than some part-time romance neither of us could maintain."

When he kissed her again, she could practically feel the gratitude.

Saying goodbye to Matt was easier than Bridget had expected. For one thing, she was surrounded by half his family and a third of hers. Sunday they all went into Boston and had brunch at Sky's family's Beacon Hill house, a nineteenth-century Georgian manse on Mount Vernon Street.

It gave Bridget a chance to look over the national historic landmark she was about to call home. After they ate, Kevin, Ryan, Sky and Erin all lingered at the massive front door as Matthew said his goodbyes and stepped out into the Beacon Hill afternoon. Amidst hugs, handshakes and words of good luck, he waved carelessly and started the walk down the hill and across the Common to Back Bay and his fifth-floor apartment.

"He added something to your vacation, didn't he," Erin asked softly.

Bridget nodded.

"Treasure that friendship, you'll never do better," Erin added as they closed the door. "Since you'll both be living in town, keep your eye on him, too. Matthew takes care of everybody but himself."

"I'm not maternal the way you are," Bridget replied.

Erin smiled. "I didn't mean that he needs a mother."

"He made it very clear that he doesn't need anything else, either."

In the intervening weeks before her permanent arrival, Bridget returned to Valley View, packed for her relocation and called each of the Atlanta-bound friends. Breaking the news about her change of plans wasn't difficult. The other women kidded her, pointing out the fact that without employment she wouldn't have added much to their financial base anyway. They all wished her well.

There'd been lots of news from Millbrook. Holly had given birth—uncomplicated and in the hospital this time—to a son, Peter Andrew Branigan. His first name was for Peter Bancroft, the guardian who raised the orphaned Branigans, the man Holly had only discovered after his death had been her father.

Bridget also heard—from Megan herself—that the on-again, off-again relationship with Jody was on

again, for good. News of Matt also came only through
her sisters. He was adjusting to his schedule and was
more enthusiastic about medicine than Erin had ever
seen him. Bridget didn't hear directly from him and
hadn't expected to. It was as clean a break as they
could make it. She knew that when he came up for air,
he would be in touch. She also knew that when that
day came, she would have to prepare herself for a different man from the rested, sensuous, uninhibited
sailor she'd known in Millbrook.

All of Bridget's chaos and adjusting was eclipsed,
however, by Erin's news. Marnie Taylor, her obstetrician, had found a second heartbeat on the fetal heart
monitor. Matt's suspicions were verified: she was carrying twins.

The morning Bridget left for Boston, Hugh
O'Connor did little to hide his delight, and his sigh of
relief was almost palpable. "Letting go of the youngest is the toughest," he whispered to his daughter as
they hugged. "I expect the others to keep an eye on
you and I expect you to lend a hand to Erin when you
can."

"I'd be happy to help Erin, but nobody needs to
keep an eye on me!"

"I only meant that when you need someone, it'll be
nice having so much family close by."

Three weeks after accepting Carla Benoit's offer,
Bridget returned to Boston. Her car was packed with
little more than clothes and memorabilia. Sky and
Ryan were on Mount Vernon Street to meet her, before leaving for a Red Sox game. Erin called from her
office, and Megan called from hers. With each, Brid-

get laughingly implored them to let her get settled and give her breathing room.

At Back Bay Associates she was assigned to work with account manager Trevor Davis as well as chief copywriter David Listro, a man in his fifties and an expert in the field. Both of them eagerly instructed her in the fine points of fund-raising. The moment she returned to Beacon Hill in the evenings—rent notices from the *Globe* in hand—she puttered around in the Greenleaf Manse, doing her best to make it feel like home. The cavernous house was pleasant enough when she rose in the morning or came home to a long summer evening. Nights, however, were a different matter. Alone upstairs, she awoke at the slightest noise, and in the antique house there were plenty. Her self-prescribed remedy was work that she brought home in her briefcase and pored over long into the night.

By the end of the first week, her family was taking her at her word and leaving her to adjust to the working world, and by then she was thoroughly enjoying herself. Friday morning as she was rinsing her breakfast dishes, the hard rap of the brass knocker made her jump. Already dressed for the office, she hurried back through the door. Mount Vernon Street at eight in the morning seemed safe enough. She hesitated, then pulled back the door. Matthew Branigan was on the granite stoop. He barely resembled the man she'd last seen in the same spot.

"Matt!"

"That bad, huh?"

She ushered him in. His green eyes were still bright, but he had a night's growth of beard and the healthy color from his sailing excursion had long been replaced by circles under his eyes. His dark disheveled hair teased the collar of his wrinkled white lab coat.

"Are you on your way to the hospital?"

He shook his head. "Just got off. I've been on call for the last twenty-four hours. It's a three-day rotation."

"Emergencies all night."

"Have you eaten?"

"I seem to recall a few tuna sandwiches. God, you look wonderful."

She glanced at her own fresh linen suit. "You should be home sleeping."

"Hell, you've been here almost a week and I haven't had a chance to welcome you. I tried half a dozen times to break away at the hospital but it was impossible."

"I didn't expect to hear from you. I know your schedule."

"I suppose you're about to leave for work?"

She nodded. "I've got time to fix you something."

"Would you?"

"Of course. Follow me out to the kitchen." She stopped. "Better still, go plunk yourself down in the library and get comfortable. I'll bring you something you can eat in there. Would you rather have breakfast or dinner?"

"Anything but tuna fish." He looked toward the room that was on the north side of the house. "I hope the shades are open. Anything resembling darkness puts me in an instant stupor.''

"You sound like a victim of sleep deprivation.''

"I am, and it's damned tougher than I thought.''

Three days of cooking for one had left Bridget with a half dozen leftovers, and thanks to the microwave oven, she was able to put together a dinner of pork chops, green beans and potatoes. She tossed a small salad, added a glass of iced tea and fifteen minutes later, walked back through the house with the meal on the tray.

Matt Branigan had pulled off his tie, lab coat and shoes and was sound asleep on the couch. She whispered his name twice before returning the meal to the refrigerator.

Bridget grabbed a cotton blanket from a spare bedroom and when he still didn't stir as she draped it over him, she left him a note telling him to reheat the dinner and make sure the door was locked when he left. She stood for a long time at the foot of the couch looking at his peaceful expression, nearly masked by fatigue. It filled her heart with yearning and she spent the entire walk across the Common to Copley Square convincing herself that the emotion was nothing more than simple compassion.

She arrived at her desk regretting the comment on locking the door. Why hadn't she thought to tell him to stay where he was? He could just as easily sleep in the Mount Vernon Street house as at his apartment. She thought of calling but didn't want to disturb him and then chided herself for putting so much energy into it. Matthew Branigan would sleep where he pleased, of that she was certain.

The first days at Back Bay Associates, she'd cut her professional teeth on a fund-raising package for a children's home in West Texas. Thursday was spent with the rest of the creative team polishing the proposal and samples of appeals that Carla would take with her Friday evening when she flew out to El Paso to present them. Bridget accepted hearty compliments on her first effort and at five-thirty when she left her desk, she was anxious to share her enthusiasm.

The Greenleaf house was empty. The blanket lay folded on the couch and in the kitchen, next to a clean plate, she found a note.

Bridget—
I did eat after all. Thanks. I'll return the favor tomorrow night if you'll take pot luck at 319 Marlborough Street. Come about six. I should be fairly coherent by then.

                                          Matt

Friday dragged. Her co-workers seemed oblivious to her daydreaming, but Bridget's rate of concentration was diminished. She left at the dot of five, which gave her just enough time to change into casual clothes, pull together samples of her first week's work, buy a handful of daisies from a vendor and walk the brick sidewalks along Beacon Street and over to Marlborough.

She buzzed his apartment from the entrance of the bow-front town house and waited, but there was no returning buzz to unlock the front door. She tried again. Nothing. She should have called and confirmed the invitation. She was dealing with an exhausted intern who might very well have been called back to the hospital on an emergency.

Bridget sat on the stoop and imagined every conceivable trauma when Matthew jogged around the corner, across the street and up over the curb.

"Bridget, what a surprise!"

She handed him the flowers as his expression shifted to doubt.

"You completely forgot!" His already flushed complexion deepened until the Branigan blush made her laugh.

"No, I didn't. I just took a little too much time for a run. Come on up." He leaned against the door and doubled over until he caught his breath.

"Out of shape even after all those hours chasing down hospital corridors?"

"It's the fatigue," he muttered. "God, it's awful."

She followed him up the five flights of steps listening to his labored breathing as she climbed. "Matthew Branigan, you're more winded than I am," she said at the top.

He nodded and unlocked the door without comment. The apartment was as she'd remembered it. Charming, cozy, furnished casually with a few nice pieces and castoffs from the Salvation Army Thrift Store. Erin's touch was long gone, although Nancy Reed's room was the way Bridget remembered it.

A small room air conditioner hummed in the living room, making the August evening bearable. Matt took a towel from the bathroom and wiped his brow.

"I'm seeing a whole new side of you," she said.

He sighed. "You're in for a shock, I'm afraid."

"Interning is tougher than you'd thought?"

"Dealing with the schedule is, yes. So far my brain is saturated and my body keeps yelling, 'Quit, you fool, give me a break!'"

"You wouldn't."

"Quit?" He shook his head. "But I'll tell you, Bridget, it's tempting. Sometimes nothing more than adrenaline and sheer defiance keeps me going. Half the time I feel like I'm suffering from Wernicke-Korsakoff's syndrome. Short-term memory loss," he added when she looked confused.

"You *did* forget this dinner invitation."

He gave her a sheepish grin.

"Then be glad I'm not some gorgeous nurse you're trying to impress. Go take a shower and I'll get things started."

He leaned over and kissed her, careful not to ruin her fresh clothes.

"Salty," she murmured.

"Sweet," he whispered back.

Nine

The shower recharged Matt long enough to salvage the evening. Bridget talked first about her job and the impossible quest to find an affordable apartment. When she'd finished, she listened with fascination to his descriptions of his first weeks in internal-medicine rotation.

This was not the Matthew she'd known in Millbrook—sexy, physical, anxious to satisfy any craving. The man who'd been immersed in the pleasures of the bogs and the bay, drifting, as she'd been, through warm days, free of obligations, was gone.

This Matt was focused the way Erin had described him years earlier. He talked of the patient load and the brutal hours, the lack of sleep and the crummy food. All of it, however, was tempered by his glowing descriptions of the practice of medicine. He described his morning rounds with the resident, the procedures, the detective work required of any doctor to treat and cure.

"It's the challenge I'd been hoping for," he continued. "Any given medical problem can be underscored by liver damage. A guy can come in with shortness of breath or pain and the workup reveals low liver function or pancreas problems unrelated to the ailment."

"Which means you have to make them well without making them more sick."

"Exactly!"

"Any regrets?" she asked as they finished dessert.

She envisioned this man she'd made love with in an orchard as he was at work. She saw him in his white coat, leading medical students along a corridor, guiding them through bedside diagnoses. It was easy to imagine him ministering alone in the middle of the night, filling out charts and prescribing treatment. What she couldn't imagine, as the evening wore on, was time devoted to anything else. He simply didn't have any to spare.

It was obvious that the intense physical relationship they'd shared so briefly was over. Matt was making that clear as much by subjects he didn't raise as those he did. Bridget berated herself for thinking about it. They'd laid the boundaries from the beginning. Did she really think she could compete with a love of medicine? Did she really think he wouldn't find someone else right under his nose at the hospital?

"Regrets," he repeated. "Look around. The apartment's a mess. Laundry's tough to do and I can't seem to get to the barber."

"You're on your own with the laundry, but if you've got a decent pair of scissors, I can cut your hair."

"Would you? Bridget, that would be fantastic!"

"It's a little thing," she laughed.

"Not when the chief of the service stares at your collar."

His comment gave her an excuse to brush the hair tickling the back of his neck. "Too shaggy for such an upstanding position? Get the scissors and I'll trim it."

He grabbed a stool from the kitchen and propped it in front of the mirror over the bureau in Nancy's room. Bridget wrapped a towel over his T-shirt. She had to fight a sudden urge to caress his shoulder. She itched to massage his neck. Instead she dabbed a small amount of water on his hair with her comb. The familiar texture of his hair tickled her palms, inciting memories so intimate her breath caught. She glanced at him in the mirror and he held her gaze in the reflection.

"You're flushed."

She busied herself with the comb. "It's a hot summer night."

"I'm glad you came over. I'm sorry I forgot. It isn't you."

She began to snip.

"Bridget?"

She looked at his concerned expression in the mirror.

"You know that, don't you?"

"Of course! Matt, you're making too much of it. I understand completely."

"Will you stay tonight?"

She took a deep breath and held it, and when she didn't reply, he cupped her cheek with his hand so that she would bend down. "Stay and let me make it up to you."

They kissed with only their lips touching; she was still holding the scissors. She welcomed his kiss hesitantly, but the feel of his tongue against hers was too wonderful to deny. Desire bolted through her until she was afraid her knees would buckle. She puckered, forcing their sensuality down to simple playfulness. The final gesture was a chaste one.

"This is a no kiss," she said gently.

He nuzzled her neck. "It didn't start out that way."

"What counts is the way it wound up, Matthew."

"You could have fooled me."

Bridget was still standing while he sat on the stool. Impulsively, she put her hand in his shaggy hair and held him against her breasts. "That's more like it," he murmured.

"Don't misread me, Doc. Perhaps I owe you an apology. I let you make love to me in Millbrook—"

"Let me? That needs a little rephrasing."

"All right, I made love with you. We made love in Millbrook because I wanted to prove to myself that Todd hadn't killed that part of me, that I was still capable of feeling whole."

"I might have bought that the first time, but not in the orchard."

"Then consider the orchard a mistake."

"The hell I will."

"You must. The truth is, both times were wonderful in their own way. But I was too raw over losing Todd, too wrapped up in getting a hold on my own emotions to think of anyone but myself. I used you to get in touch with my feelings," she managed, emotion rising in her throat.

"Then it worked damn well."

"At what expense? I used you, Matt. I don't want to jump in and out of bed with you or anyone. I'm not that type of person. I'd hate myself and you, too, eventually. It was wrong of me at the bogs and it's wrong now. Don't pretend you can't see it."

"I'm not pretending anything. I'm feeling human for the first time in weeks. That desire—what I want with you—is real. If you'll give me your hand, I'll show you." He tugged her wrist in the direction of his lap but she pulled her hand back.

"Don't joke about this."

"Do you see me laughing?"

"Matt, medicine's all consuming for you and that's the way it should be. That's the way it *has* to be. We talked about it. We've talked it to death. I'm sure there are other women eager to make you happy. I don't want to be anybody's one-night stand, but especially not yours. We're family now. We'll overlap in Millbrook."

"I like the part about overlapping."

"Joke if you must."

"It helps, but it doesn't make me want you any less."

She ached to add that it didn't make her want him any less, either. Instead, she stood behind him and snipped the scissors open and closed. "Let's get down to business," she added.

"It doesn't feel like business when your hands are in my hair."

"Shall we go see if a barber's open at nine o'clock on a Saturday night?"

He put his hands over hers as they rested on his shoulders. "Stay."

"Behave."

He yawned. "What choice do I have?"

She snipped the air again. "Very little."

When she'd clipped and trimmed enough to get him through another few weeks, Bridget declared the haircut finished and watched Matt cock his head as he looked closely in the mirror. "Yet another of your talents. Somehow I've got to stop thinking about the other ones."

She ignored the innuendo. "Haircutting's not my forte, but it'll keep your superiors happy. You do look more like a physician and less like a rock star—an exhausted physician."

Matt stifled another yawn. "Sorry."

"Let me call a cab and I'll be on my way."

Matt slung his arm across her shoulder as they went back into the living room. "Would it do any good for me to try a little seduction?"

"No."

"What if I begged?"

Bridget laughed, but she spent a long time looking at the depth in his green eyes before shaking her head.

"The position we're in forces me to choose between lover and friend."

"Then at least tell me it was a tough choice."

She kissed him quickly. "Tougher than you know."

Matt patted his heart. "Hope springs eternal."

Sunday morning, armed with a baby gift for Drew and Holly and the Sunday *Globe* rental listings, Bridget decided on an impromptu visit to Millbrook. It would be cooler out of the city and she needed the company. The ride was hot and she longed not for air conditioning in her car, but Matt beside her.

She stayed up half the night in the cavernous bedroom of the cavernous Beacon Hill house. Desire had torn at her from the moment Matt had jogged around the corner. She'd even been a little hurt at his casual air in their first minutes together. What had made her turn him down? What had made her lie to him when what she ached for was what he wanted, too?

Todd Harrison, old wounds and self-doubts had played no part in her decision to make love with Matthew Branigan. *Decision* hadn't even played a part. Matthew Branigan had enveloped her. His compassion, humor, kindness and consideration had become tangible when he'd held her. She'd made love with him both times because it was the most compelling, natural, instinctively right emotion she'd ever felt. So right that as she lay in bed and analyzed it, she was frightened.

She shuddered as unexpressed desire still teased her body. Todd had been right to break the engagement. What she'd felt for him had none of the depth or conviction she felt for Matt. Matt said he wanted occasional sex with her; he needed her to be willing to accept the status quo. She'd lied to him and only now did she realize why. It was the only protection she had from what she ached to share with him, which was so much more than he had to give.

Beyond the physical desire, she wanted to hear more of his life, more stories about his patients and the daily challenges he faced. After a week at her own job, Bridget had much to share, as well, most of it barely touched on the night before.

It would have been so easy to have stayed with him, to have thrown caution to the wind and followed her own desire. Moment to moment she couldn't think of anyone more passionate and desirable. However, it wasn't the moments that worried her. It was the stretches between, the long empty days and nights when they went their separate ways, when another woman whose free time might coincide with his would do just as well. She couldn't give herself so completely just for fun and need. She couldn't be part of Matt's life on those terms, and those terms were all Matthew Branigan could offer.

Millbrook was alive with activity. Bridget stayed long enough at Drew's to admire the baby as he slept in his cradle. Holly opened the present and hugged her. "Having all you O'Connors around is like another batch of family. I was an only child and marrying into this clan makes up for lost time in one fell swoop!"

Bridget raised a finger. "I'm not part of this clan."

"Maybe not officially, but there's still room. We have two slots open, although Megan seems to have filled the other one nicely."

"I never though she'd accept Jody on his own terms."

"Jody compromised. Love does that. Giving up law altogether made no sense. He's a perfect combination of knowledge and practical application where the environment is concerned. There'll still be time for representing cranberry growers and growing the little berries, too." The women walked back onto the porch. "That leaves one more."

"Holly—"

"I know, I know. You and Matt are just friends and it's none of my business."

"True."

"That never stopped me before."

"You've got your hands full right here. Don't get any ideas."

"Matthew needs somebody to watch out for him, the way he used to watch out for your sister."

"What Matt needs is sleep and lots of it."

"Boring existence, all that devotion and medicine."

"That's how doctors are made."

"If the timing were different would there be anything between you two?"

"The timing *isn't* different. There's nothing either of us can do to to change that."

"Don't be so sure. Fate has a way of stepping in when you least expect it. I'm a perfect example of that. I only came to Millbrook to sell my property. If

I hadn't had the chimney fire that forced me to stay on longer and deal with Drew, I'd probably be back in Philadelphia happily putting my elusive MBA degree to work there."

"A chimney fire wouldn't make a difference in my situation."

"Of course it wouldn't, but my point is that something else, something totally unexpected like that, might change the complexion of your situation."

Bridget touched her cheeks facetiously. "My complexion's fine."

Holly hugged her again. "I know. When you talk about Dr. Branigan you positively glow."

Bridget had no intention of glowing, in front of Holly or anyone else. Megan and Erin were glowing enough to light the bogs. After all the turmoil and consternation, her middle sister was smug in her happiness and more settled than Bridget had ever seen her.

Early in the afternoon, the three sisters ate a picnic lunch together and Bridget was left with the indelible impression that all was right in both their worlds. Erin had gone from accepting the idea of twins to real excitement.

"Kevin can't wait, either. It will give us a complete family all in one fell swoop."

Before she headed back to Beacon Hill, Bridget read the Boston rental notices out loud. "Nothing," she muttered to her sisters. "The only affordable apartments are in neighborhoods too unsafe to live alone."

"It's time to consider roommates," Erin added. "Maybe Matt could post a notice in the hospital or at the med school."

"You're overlooking Matt's apartment. He's got plenty of room now and he's hardly ever there. You've said so yourself." Megan added.

"Not an option," Bridget snapped.

Erin patted her shoulder. "I've said so from the beginning. Don't give in to temptation."

"He's not my type. I'm not even attracted to him."

"I meant the temptation to move into my old room or Nancy's, Bridge," she corrected, her eyes sparkling.

Bridget returned to Mount Vernon Street early to avoid the rush of traffic returning from Cape Cod. She took a walk after an early supper and chatted with half a dozen neighbors out enjoying the end of the weekend. For good measure she also called a few college friends who'd settled in town and let the word out that she was interested in sharing an apartment. In time she was sure something would come her way.

A week went by and nothing did, then another. Late in August her work schedule was given over to creating a Christmas fund-raising campaign for a neighborhood health clinic. It was tough to find the right mood with the air conditioner humming and the staff in short sleeves. Bridget sat in on the creative department meeting with David, jotting down any number of ideas as they popped into her head. As she listened to the financial woes and descriptions of destitute patients, she thought of Matt, busy at that very moment with his own heavy caseload.

The executive session was over at lunch and she settled at her word processor only to be interrupted by

Hilary. As usual she still looked immaculate. "Not the kind of weather conducive to a Christmas campaign," she said as she came into Bridget's office.

"I suppose in December we'll be writing for spring and summer."

"Absolutely." Hilary pulled up a chair and made herself comfortable. "I've come in with another proposition. Carla's wrapped up the Texas account and I think I'd like to hand this project over to her."

"You don't think Dave and I can handle it?"

"That's not it at all, but I've got something else in mind for you guys. We've been hired by an area hospital to guide a massive year-end appeal. They want to do it in-house and need guidance rather than a complete package. David's the man to work with their department, and I'd like you to go along for the education. You'll be a help and I'm sure what you pick up can be invaluable."

"On-the-job training?"

"Precisely."

"I'd love to as long as somebody takes over here."

"That part's all set."

"Who's the client?"

"New England Regional Hospital. You and David are to begin first thing Wednesday morning, eight-thirty in their administration offices. Do you know the hospital? It's smack in the middle of the medical complex on Brewer Street. Go through the doctor's entrance. The administration offices are right in front. They'll arrange for parking passes, although the MBTA Red Line stops at the corner."

"New England Regional?"

"Might as well start you at the top."

Long after Hilary had returned to her own office, Bridget sat at her desk conjuring up visions of Matthew Branigan, M.D., lurking at her desk, stethoscope in his pocket, the irrepressible look of desire in his eyes.

Despite the fantasy, she didn't call to tell him the news. She wasn't sure of his hours and didn't want to risk waking him from what little sleep he could grab. More to the point, she wasn't at all sure how he would react or how she even wanted him to react. It was difficult enough knowing he was in the same city. How on earth would she be able to concentrate knowing he was in the same building?

Wednesday morning she dressed for air-conditioned business in a cotton skirt, linen blouse and blazer, then nearly sweltered on the MBTA as she crossed the city with hundreds of other commuters. The blazer was relegated to her arm before she left the mass-transit system. From the T station, New England Regional Hospital loomed at the top of a small incline, which at its founding in the first quarter of the nineteenth century had been a grassy knoll. The original building of brick and granite added dignity to its modern neighbors. Since its founding by Harvard University, it had been in the forefront of medical research and treatment. As Bridget walked up to the entrance, the idea that she could offer even a modicum of professional advice seemed ludicrous. As she entered, she made a vow to keep her eyes open and her mouth shut. Matthew Branigan was opening the door from the other side, on his way out.

"Bridget!"

"Matt!" He had the usual twenty-four-hour growth of beard and circles under his eyes.

"I *thought* it was you coming up the steps." He looked her up and down. "Are you sick?"

"Working."

"Here?"

"The public relations department hired Back Bay Associates for some consulting work for the next few weeks. They sent me along to soak up the experience. You're on your way home?"

"I got off an hour ago but I had a patient in distress so I stuck around until she stabilized. You look as gorgeous as ever," he added, rubbing his brow as if admitting defeat.

"As overworked interns go, you do, too." She touched his collar. "Haircut's holding up."

"I could use another. It's been a while."

"Has it?"

Her reply seemed to disappoint him. "It was at least two strokes, half a dozen coronary bypasses and a liver transplant ago."

"Surgery rotation?"

"Intensive care."

"You could use some yourself."

He touched her cheek. "You don't know how much."

"That's not what I meant."

Matt yawned and looked as though he could have fallen asleep there against the door. "Maybe not, but that's how I feel." He closed his eyes. "Except at the moment I'm more desperate for sleep than sex."

"You need it more, too."

"Somehow, I knew you'd say that."

She laughed. "After all this time, I'm sure I've been replaced."

"You know me that well?"

"I know your needs and your philosophy."

"Would you care to enlighten me over lunch when I'm back on the floor?"

"I'd like that," she replied.

"Then it's a deal. How about my first day back on rotation?"

"Wouldn't that be Saturday?"

"Saturday?" He yawned again. "You're right. I'll be working but you'll be off. I come off the shift Monday. How about Monday?"

"All right. How about breakfast? I could come in early."

"Seven-thirty?"

"Sure."

"Then we'll try Monday. Right here." He started to leave but she touched his arm.

While he waited, Bridget rifled through her purse and wrote out the time, date and place on a scrap of paper. "Pin it where you'll see it."

His smile was rueful. "It's no joke, I can't remember anything. I'll need this."

"I thought by now maybe you'd get used to the fatigue."

Matt cupped her cheek. "The human body, psyche included, has requirements in order to function properly. Deprivation plays havoc in all kinds of ways."

She put her hand over his. "It *is* sleep you're referring to," she commented skeptically.

"Among other things."

She paused before finally asking what she burned to know. "Matt, isn't there someone else now? Since the orchard? Surely since that night I cut your hair and told you—"

He pushed back his lab coat and shoved his hands into his pockets. "Bridget, I'm dead on my feet. We'll talk about this another time. I'll see you next Monday." Abruptly, he turned and left.

Bridget stayed at the open door long enough to watch him walk into the sunshine. A beam of light streamed off the crown of his head and over his shoulder. The thought that Matthew Branigan might not have found someone else stirred her as much as the simple act of touching his hand. "Ships in the night," she whispered, knowing it would be five days until they would meet again.

Ten

―――

Bridget's introduction to the working of a hospital PR department filled her day. Knowing Matt wasn't there increased her efficiency and she concentrated entirely on the project at hand, impressed with the colleagues she'd been assigned to.

When not on the job, she was determined not to spend all her free time in Millbrook. Rushing back to be with her sisters was a crutch she wanted to avoid. Instead, she called her college friends on the pretext of asking about apartments and was immediately invited to join them for Labor Day weekend at a rented cottage on the North Shore. It was just the contact she needed to broaden her social life and her outlook.

When the phone rang after dinner, she expected it to be one of her sisters, but, over the static of hospital background noise, she heard Matt's deep voice. "Bridget?"

"Matt? Are you at the hospital?"

"The ICU patients are all in critical condition. I've got one that needed monitoring."

"I'm sorry."

"So am I." His voice was flat. "You're going to think I'm crazy, but I'm calling to see if I ran into you this morning on the hospital steps."

"You don't remember?"

"That much I *do* remember. But it didn't seem possible and frankly, I've been dreaming about you a lot lately. This seemed like it might have been something my overtaxed subconscious conjured up."

"It wasn't a dream. My firm's doing some consulting with your PR office. You asked me to meet you for breakfast on Monday. I wrote it down so you wouldn't forget."

"I'll find it."

"Matt, I'm worried about you."

"Hell, one of the interns coming off twenty-four hours in the emergency ward fell asleep on her three-block MBTA ride and woke up in Quincy. We're all like this. It goes with the territory."

"It's not healthy."

"You've been worried?"

"I've been thinking about what you have to deal with, yes."

"There's another reason I called. Damn! I'm being paged. Gotta go. I found you an apartment. I'll show you. Lunch tomorrow. I'll come to your office. Gotta go—it's a code." The phone line went dead, and she was left to envision Matt racing down the corridor on the way to meet the emergency.

At twelve-fifteen the next day, Bridget was poring over the hospital's direct-mail solicitations from previous years when Matt appeared in the doorway. "Ready to go take a look?"

"You're here!"

"You forgot?"

"Of course not, but I never thought *you'd* remember. I wasn't expecting you. I've got an awful lot to do. I don't suppose we could postpone this till tonight?"

"Not with my schedule."

She stood up. "You've slept."

"You see an improvement, I assume."

"No whiskers, the circles under your eyes aren't so deep. Matt, I worry about you."

They'd turned the corner in the empty corridor and he stopped long enough to look at her. "You've said that before. You don't need to, but it means a lot."

"Maybe if I knew the other interns, if I had some basis for comparison, I wouldn't stew, but you're not the man I knew in Millbrook."

"I told you I wouldn't be."

"I know." She leaned back against the wall. "But I suspect this internship is more overwhelming than even you expected."

Matt leaned toward her slowly, cocked his head and kissed her. There wasn't enough force or pressure in it for her to resist. And as usual, she didn't want to. She put her arm lightly across his shoulder and returned the soft, sensual pressure of the mouth she adored.

"You're not to do that," she whispered when he'd pulled back.

"I try not to."

A nurse in her mid-fifties crossed their path. "There's a supply closet around the corner, if you need privacy, Dr. Branigan."

"I'm saving that for you and me, D'Allesandro."

"Watch out for that one," she replied to Bridget. "He's all talk. No action."

"I'm waiting for you to put down the sphygmomanometers and the IV drips," Matt scoffed.

"Every excuse in the book," she finished with a grin.

Matt put his arm around Bridget's waist and ushered her toward the hospital entrance. "Angela D'Allesandro, the angel of intensive care."

"I'll bet she's seen it all in you guys, year after year."

"She'd be the first to tell you."

"While you're here, do you want to check on that patient you were monitoring last night?"

"No."

"I know how precious your time is. I don't mind waiting. Go ahead if you need to."

"No need, she's in the morgue."

"Matt!"

"Forty-one, mother of three. We lost her last night."

They left the air-conditioned building for the oppressive air of the humid city and Bridget took Matt's arm as they crossed the parking lot. "I wish I'd known."

"Why? There was nothing to be done that we hadn't tried already." His voice was tight with frustration.

"I didn't mean for the patient. I meant for you."

"It's so damned frustrating," he continued, almost to himself. "We're surrounded by the most technically advanced equipment in the world—we've got the best medical minds in the country and what it all boils down to is illusion, sleight of hand. After days of treating every symptom, monitoring every function, in the end we're just fending off death for a few more hours."

"Matthew, I'm sure you did everything you could."

"Sure did. Wasn't enough."

"There must be some comfort in knowing you've done everything you could."

"Comfort? We worked on her. No one slept—no one ate. She cheated us out of victory. She cheated us out of any reward for extraordinary effort, superhuman effort. I tried to find a pulse even when the monitor told me there wasn't one. 'You can't be dead,' I must have said that fifty times. There's no comfort Bridget, just anger, and the worst part is that it isn't clean anger. It's fuzzy. I'm angry at myself, at medicine, at nature. Death won and I lost, and in the ICU it's like that day in and day out. Hour in and hour out, for that matter."

The profound change in Matt deepened Bridget's concern. He talked as he drove with her through the streets to the Back Bay section she was familiar with. She had no idea where the apartment he was to show her was located. He had yet to mention it. At the moment, although it was the point of their trip, it seemed inconsequential.

She tried to recall the details of Matt's intern rotation. He'd described it so enthusiastically in the earlier weeks. He'd been brimming with hope and determination as if he wanted only the chance to rise to the challenge of such grave medical situations.

She realized now how much of the enthusiasm came from theory. Practice was a very different situation. "Do you talk about this with the others? Aren't there five of you?" she asked.

"It would be unbearable without them."

"Be grateful for that support. At least the stress is shared. Matt, promise me you'll talk this out with your team when you're with them. Promise me you won't carry it all by yourself."

"I can't make promises to you, Bridget."

"They only concern your own welfare. I'm only asking for you to think about yourself."

"This stage of doctoring wasn't designed with that in mind. You're not in medicine so you don't understand. I shouldn't have brought it up. Let's change the subject. I never meant to dwell on it in the first place."

"I'm glad you brought it up. You needed to."

"Maybe, maybe not. I also need to get away from it."

By the time he'd inched through the Beacon Street traffic, his mood had brightened. She suspected that he forced himself, but he abruptly changed the subject from the ICU to Nurse D'Allesandro. According to Matt, she actually *had* caught two amorous interns making love in the supply closet.

"How embarrassing!"

"I guess so—but it turned out they were newlyweds on different shifts."

Bridget laughed and accepted his change of topic—and tone. Survival as a physician depended on the ability to put the trauma aside. She knew that, but she also knew that suppressing the stress would only lead to trouble.

"A few stolen moments between the towels and sheets was their substitute for a honeymoon."

"And Nurse D'Allesandro?"

"She had maintenance make up a sign that said Honeymoon Suite and stuck it on the door."

They'd reached Matt's neighborhood and he drove the car off the street and up into the alley that separated the backs of the town houses lining Beacon and Marlborough streets, spaces now used for private parking.

"Isn't this the back of your building?"

"Yes. I meant to explain everything on the way over."

"Matt, I hope you're not up to your old tricks."

"Tricks?"

"Don't play innocent. I'm referring to the last time I was here. You'd barely take no for an answer."

"Meaning?"

"Meaning you should be upstairs sound asleep, not priming me with stories about Nurse D'Allesandro and duping me into thinking you've found me an apartment. I suspect all you're offering is one of your spare bedrooms."

"You've got me all figured out?"

"Obviously."

"Humor me. Since we're here, come on in. You've got lots of time left in your lunch hour. I'll make you a peanut-butter sandwich."

She climbed the stairs with him and when they'd reached the fourth landing, he paused and knocked on one of the two closed apartment doors. A blond woman about their age opened it and smiled.

"Matt, for once you're right on time." She stuck out her hand. "You must be Bridget O'Connor. I knew your sister briefly when she lived upstairs. Come on in. I don't know how much the doctor's told you, but I sure appreciate what you're doing for me."

"What I'm doing?" Bridget looked back at Matt, who was about to climb the last flight of stairs.

"I'm sure you'll want to take a look. Come on in," the woman continued.

Matt grinned. "I never got around to the details. Bridget, this is Amanda Butler. She's a graduate piano student at the Boston Conservatory and has just been given the chance to study in Paris. Get acquainted. I'll whip up that sandwich. Come on up when you're finished." He winked and disappeared into the rooms above, which embarrassed Bridget further.

Amanda lead her inside. "I'll be leaving right after Labor Day for a semester, two if I'm lucky. It's all last minute because the grant was given to another student who has a family emergency and had to back out. I've got to sublet this apartment, but I hate the thought of leaving it to just anybody."

"I can see why," Bridget replied. Unlike the rooms upstairs, Amanda's apartment was furnished with eclectic items of obvious value. The small living area held a spinet piano, chintz-covered love seat and club chairs. A drop-leaf table was tucked up against the counter that separated the galley kitchen. An even smaller bedroom was just large enough for a double bed and dresser.

When Bridget finally left Amanda, she'd nearly exhausted her lunch hour. Matt's apartment door was open and she called him as she went in. There was no answer. A peanut-butter sandwich, some fig bars and hastily peeled carrot sticks were on a plate.

She found Matt asleep on his unmade bed. He lay on his back, still fully dressed right down to his shoes. Bridget lingered over him, studying the exhaustion in his face and the peaceful rise and fall of his chest. The temptation to join him was heightened by physical stirring in places too dangerous for her to dwell on. Instead Bridget tiptoed out of his bedroom, made sure she had enough money with her for cab fare, wrapped her lunch in a paper towel and left him a note.

Dr. Branigan,
Forgive me for my conclusion-jumping. Amanda's offer is too good to pass up. I'm subletting beginning the first week in September. Thanks for thinking of me.

Get some sleep
Bridget

At the end of the Labor Day weekend, Bridget had set a small goal for herself. She intended to devote the month of September to getting her life in order. In theory it didn't seem difficult. Her job was going well and the assignment at New England Regional Hospital was nearly over.

By working on the site, she'd gained an invaluable perspective of care-giving from an administrative point of view. The pragmatism required in hospital management was softened by what she observed in Matt and the stories he shared with her. The combination made her writing more effective and added a dimension to her work for which she was congratulated.

Matthew himself was another matter. It hadn't taken more than a hand from Amanda and a thank-you to Sky and Ryan for Bridget to move her belongings from Beacon Hill to Marlborough Street. She'd settled in right on schedule. She was now working and living in the same buildings as he did, and she saw no more of him than she had while living on Mount Vernon Street.

He had shown up for their Monday-morning breakfast date only to be paged to ICU. They were invited to Peter Branigan's christening, and Bridget had great hopes of spending time with Matt there, including time alone on the drive down and back. At the last minute, one of his patient's developed ventricular tachycardia and the life-threatening situation forced her to attend by herself.

They were ships in the night, all right, ships barely cruising the same channel. She compensated by focusing on her own schedule, grateful that she'd had the good sense to back off from any physical relationship with him. It was tough enough being his friend.

Bridget was looking forward to the approaching autumn when Boston and Millbrook would be at their best. At the baptismal celebration, Branigan talk centered on the coming harvest. It promised to be good one as long as the bogs were carefully monitored during frost warnings. Lack of sleep went hand-in-glove with the season.

"Once a year you all get to be as exhausted as Matt," she told Kevin, Drew, Ryan, Sean and Jody—who were anxious for news of their brother.

Since Erin was carrying twins, which increased the likelihood of a premature delivery, she, too, was being monitored very carefully. At every opportunity Kevin was teased by his brothers about the timing. Cranberry growers knew better than to have their children born in the fall. October was becoming as likely a month for the babies' arrivals as November. Bridget spent the visit wishing Matt had been there, knowing how much he needed the relaxed and loving atmosphere.

Her life now included the college friends she'd touched base with and associates from work, which balanced her family connections in Millbrook. Megan's and Erin's lives were so full, they didn't do any of the hovering she'd feared. She had freedom, responsibility and the love of her family at her fingertips.

On a warm evening, with time on her hands, Bridget took the MBTA's Red Line into Cambridge and shopped in Harvard Square. She was on Brattle Street when the sound of her name made her turn. Todd Harrison was at the curb.

"Bridget! I thought you were in Atlanta."

Her heart had jumped at the unexpected sight of him, but the emotion was simple surprise. She shook her head. "I got a job in Boston." She offered bits of information, and he asked her to elaborate. Because he was genuinely interested and Bridget wanted to make clear that she was fine and doing well, the conversation continued as they walked. Forty minutes later, over a cup of coffee, she listened, too, as Todd described his first weeks in graduate school.

His rampant enthusiasm reminded her of Matt's early days and she wondered if Todd might find himself grappling with reality in a few weeks, as well. No lives hung in the balance in architecture. She wanted to tell him how lucky he was.

They parted as friends and after asking about her sisters and Kevin Branigan, all of whom he'd met the previous Christmas, Bridget and Todd went their separate ways. She left feeling free.

The only aspect of her life that she considered out of balance was her relationship with Matt, or her lack of one. His depression and frustration had shocked her enough so that she still mulled over the conversation. She saw him for five minutes on the front stoop as she left for work one morning and he came home from jogging. They spent another ten minutes together when she'd finished her last lunch at the hospital and he was in the cafeteria to pick up a sandwich. He looked rested, if disheveled.

"How are things in ICU?"

"Life or death, as usual."

"The rotation's almost over, as I recall."

"To be replaced by emergency ward."

"Just as bad?"

"High risk, low reward."

"When do you ever get the rewards?"

He yawned. "On these rotations? When somebody survives."

"Are you surviving?"

"Barely." He turned the sandwich over in his hand.

"Is that breakfast, lunch or dinner?"

"I can't remember. Doesn't pass for much of any category, does it?"

"No, it doesn't. When can I feed you?"

"Feed me? A real meal. I've forgotten what they taste like."

"They taste like fresh vegetables or tangy chicken, a pasta salad or properly cooked eggs and a muffin with Millbrook jam."

"You're bringing tears to my eyes."

"Name the time." She brushed his collar. "We'll trim your hair, too."

"Saturday's my next swing day. I'm due back here at seven Sunday morning so I should be in fairly respectable shape. Noon?"

"Saturday, it is."

Late September wasn't noted for its rain, but Saturday a bank of clouds hung over the city, swept in from the sea. Bridget's little apartment sparkled in the gray light and smelled of the now-cooling grilled chicken she'd cooked. Amanda Butler's taste suited her perfectly and the small scale of the apartment was far more comfortable for a single person than Sky's Beacon Hill house.

When the front door buzzer sounded just before twelve, Bridget went to the speaker, thinking Matt might have been jogging and forgotten his key.

"It's Todd, may I come up?"

She hesitated. "For a minute. I'm expecting company."

He appeared moments later looking yachty in damp khakis with a foul-weather slicker over his arm. She took the jacket into the bathroom to spare Amanda's carpet the raindrops dripping off the hem.

"I was at the library in Copley Square and that gave me the excuse to come see your digs." He glanced around the room. "Great setup for a sublet. You sure got lucky. You won't believe what I'm putting up with in Cambridge."

"You described it the other night."

"So I did. Something smells great."

"Lunch. I'm feeding a friend."

"Bad timing, I guess. I won't stay. I just wanted to tell you that you look great and I'm glad things are going well. Boston suits you."

"Thanks."

He paused. "I'm sorry things didn't work out for us. I hope—"

"Todd, you were absolutely right to break the engagement. You were smarter than I to recognize that what we felt for each other wasn't the real thing. It wouldn't have lasted forever."

"You believe that now, too?"

"Completely. Marriage would have been a disaster."

A lighthearted knock on the door finished the conversation, and Todd stepped aside while Bridget opened it. Matt was in the hall in ratty jeans, bare chested, towel around his neck, scissors in hand. Shock registered in his face and he flushed as he looked at Todd.

"I'm early. I thought you might want to cut my hair first so I can take a shower. Am I interrupting?"

"Not at all. This is Todd Harrison. Todd, this is my neighbor, Matt Branigan."

Todd shook his hand. "Branigan? You must be the intern. I met your brother Kevin last Christmas at the O'Connors's." He looked at Bridget. "You didn't mention that he lived in the building."

"Matt found me the apartment."

"We Branigans like to keep an eye on O'Connor women."

"So I understand."

Bridget went into the bathroom and came back with Todd's slicker. "Thanks for stopping by."

"It was good to see you, again, Bridge."

When he'd left, Bridget followed Matt upstairs into his apartment. The stool was still in front of the mirror in Nancy's room where Matt had left it. Hair clippings, however, had been swept up.

"Todd Harrison," Matt said.

"The same. I ran into him in Cambridge the other night."

"And survived, obviously."

She smiled at his unreadable expression. "Way back in April, it was you who told me I would."

"Way back in April you looked as though you might not."

"And now?"

He shrugged and sat on the stool. "Now you look like the cat that ate the canary."

"Do I?"

"Smug."

"I feel good."

Matt caught his breath and sighed as Bridget adjusted the towel and began to snip. "How good? You've seen him a couple of times already."

"I feel like I'm in control of my life."

"How long did the ex-fiancé stay?"

Bridget looked at Matt in the mirror. His expectant features weren't nearly as drawn as the last time she'd seen him. He'd slept and shaved, and she'd wondered just how feisty he was feeling. "Long enough," she replied.

"How long was long enough?" he muttered.

"You're not going to quit, are you? I'm entitled to my private life. I'm not a patient you have to do a history workup on."

"I've seen what a broken heart can do to you, Bridget. Do you think it's wise to get involved with him all over again, even if you think you can handle it?"

"I've seen him twice! We're not involved."

"Yet."

"Matthew! Not too long ago you wanted me to jump back into bed with you. I don't recall much concern then about what might happen to my heart or the fear of my getting *involved*."

"I've left you alone since then, haven't I?"

"Of course, but I just assumed your schedule—"

"I listened to what you told me, Bridget. You used me to get back in touch with yourself, to prove there was life after Harrison."

"And there is."

"Good. I won't be selfish enough to keep you from it."

"But you *do* feel qualified to comment on it."

"Well, somebody *has* to."

Eleven

Hold still!'' Bridget snapped as Matt moved his head to look at her. She put her hands over his ears and swiveled him back into position. "Matthew Branigan, it takes every ounce of energy you have to take care of your own life. Don't fuss over mine."

"I've got opinions. That's not fussing."

"Keep them to yourself."

She finished trimming the back of his neck and ears. "Your bangs and the stuff on top could use some attention, too."

"Fix it, I trust you."

She stood in front of him and began to work from the crown of his head forward. She also worked at ignoring the developing urge to kiss him.

"There are thousands of men in this town with the

appeal of Todd Harrison. Any one of them would suit you fine."

"Thank you. I'll remember that when I go out man hunting."

"Treat it as a joke, if you like, but you're vulnerable. Todd types sneak up on you."

"Todd Harrison didn't sneak up on me. We were friends for quite a while *first*. We did everything properly and that includes marriage plans. Perhaps you're putting yourself in that category? Our little escapade last June certainly snuck up on me, and there wasn't a thing proper about it."

"Should I have proposed? Can you imagine marriage under these circumstances?"

"No. Even being friends with you takes scheduling."

"And schedules are useless half the time."

"If that's your point, then I agree. It's a very good thing we're not married. It might be nice to be friends, though."

"I'd like to think we are. I've got damn few at the moment other than my colleagues."

"I could use one myself," she said with a smile.

"Everything that happened in Millbrook snuck up on me, too. I was as vulnerable as you. Sometimes at three in the morning when the rest of the world's asleep and I'm called out of bed for the third time, sometimes when I have vending machine crackers for dinner, sometimes I think June was the last time I felt anything close to happiness. I know June was the last time I felt human."

"Then you're forgetting, Matt. You're forgetting how much you wanted this. From the moment I met you at the wedding, you wrapped me in your enthusiasm and excitement."

"Did I?"

"Yes, and it was impressive. You were ready for this. You knew it would be tough, but you were ready. Everytime you talked about medicine you made it come alive for me."

"I've lost it."

Bridget finished and laid the scissors on the bureau. "It isn't lost. You've put it aside. Everyone who knows you, everybody who loves you can see what a wonderful doctor you are. ICU rotation is almost over. There'll be relief."

He put his hand through his hair and pulled away the towel. "I swore I'd never get impersonal, that a patient would never just be a bunch of symptoms, a chart workup." He sighed. "But there's so much risk at extending yourself. You offer hope to the patient, to their families because somebody's color looks better or their vital signs improve and wham! In the course of a day, it all goes down the tubes, time and time again. You can't become attached to patients without losing a part of yourself in the process. The alternative is to turn into some kind of technocrat, a whiz with the machines and gadgets we have that extend and improve life, who doesn't get involved beyond recording results."

"Matt, even I know there's a middle ground. You'll find your equilibrium."

"I'm glad you're sure of that. The lack of control feels like being shaken upside down."

"You're drained emotionally from what you're learning."

"What I'm learning is that there are no absolutes, not even death. Patients defy the odds to the other extreme, as well. Men and women you never thought would see the daylight walk out with years left to them. I inserted my first pacemaker yesterday. The senior resident talked me through it, but I did the whole damn thing myself." He raised his hands. "I shook and my own heart was in my throat, but I did it and the guy's stable. I can't even describe the feeling when the patient you're working on goes from having an unreadable blood pressure right up the scale or when somebody finds a pulse."

"Euphoric?"

"Till the guy in the next bed codes out on you."

"I'm sorry it's such a seesaw."

Matt got up from the stool and left the room with Bridget following. At the door to the bathroom, he turned around. "Hope becomes intoxicating, but the highs and lows are so extreme and so emotionally exhausting, you stop daring to hope." He turned on the shower.

"You stop thinking of the patients as people," she reiterated.

"They become strokes or GI problems or whatever else it is that's brought them there." He closed the door as he finished the sentence.

Bridget swept up the hair and straightened the room, then went downstairs to her apartment. She left the door open.

Fifteen minutes later a freshly scrubbed, cleanly dressed and apologetic Matthew Branigan came into the living room and closed the door behind him.

"Lunch will be ready in a little bit," Bridget said from the sink.

Matt came next to her. "I'm sorry. I never said a word about the haircut or the fact that I was about to get in the shower. I'm losing it, Bridget."

She looked hard into his eyes. "What you're losing is touch with the rest of the world. When was the last time you took a walk? Not a jog, a walk over these streets you love, along that river?"

"God knows."

"Lunch can wait."

"It's pouring."

"It's a drizzle. Rain won't hurt an old cranberry grower like you and a dairy farmer like me."

The rain was closer to a downpour than a drizzle, but they started off, each buckled into foul-weather slickers, hoods and gum-soled boots.

"Matthew, have you taken the time to analyze the fact that this depression is exacerbated by living alone? You don't have anybody at home to bounce it off. Not only that, but isn't this the first time in your life you've ever lived by yourself?"

"Yes."

"Pretty lousy timing. Loneliness can make any problem worse."

"Bridget, I don't have time to be lonely. I'm only home to sleep, study and get a quick haircut. Besides, if I invited you to move in, you'd turn me down."

"Don't change the subject—and keep me out of it. I'm very happy where I am."

"You brought it up."

"I meant that it's important to talk this out, Matt. Talk to the interns sharing the rotation, talk to the nurses." She hesitated then added, "Find yourself a woman who knows what you're going through, another doctor or a nurse."

"Frankly, I don't know how the nurses can stand it. They deal with this stress. They can't even hide behind impersonal medicine because they *are* the care givers. They're the ones who soothe and comfort and expend all that emotional energy."

"Empathy from a doctor! They must think you're pretty terrific."

"I take out my frustrations on them half the time. Not that I don't get it right back. It can be an armed camp when the pressure's intense."

"But there must be one or two willing to listen," Bridget added.

"One or two."

A tiny twinge of jealousy stabbed her. "I'm sure one or two of the romantically inclined have been eager to spend some time in the supply closet with you."

"That's reserved for honeymooners."

"I thought for sure once I moved in below you, I'd hear two sets of footsteps climbing the stairs in the middle of the night occasionally. You're being very discreet."

"I'm never home."

They crossed Back Bay, avoiding puddles, hunkering when the wind blew. The city was nearly theirs and although the weather gave no sign of improving, they headed for the bank of the Charles River. As they walked, Bridget took the time to point out landmarks she wasn't sure about, which changed the subject. In their ten-minute walk they'd moved from medicine to Matthew's sex life to historic landmarks.

They read the historic plaques and stood, dripping, looking at the Hatch Shell, home of the outdoor Boston Pops concerts. They watched the Red Line trains cross the Charles into Cambridge.

"'The Hub of the Universe,'" she said.

"So they tell me. I know the medical community thinks so."

"Don't lose sight of that. You're part of it."

"I'm shackled to it."

"Right now you are. Don't forget that you're the future, too. Down the road, Matthew Branigan, M.D., will be part of the reason Boston medicine is world famous."

Matt turned and looked at her. The rain had settled into a fine mist and she could see droplets of water that clung to his eyelashes. "You really believe in me, don't you?" he asked.

"Of course."

"'Of course.' Blind faith—just like my brothers."

"Certainly not. A long time ago Kevin and the older ones saw your potential. They groomed you and sacrificed for you because they knew you had what it took to be a doctor, Matt. I can see it, too."

Impulsively, she grabbed fistfuls of his hood in either hand and stared at him, nose to nose. "It's just buried under fatigue, self-doubt, discouragement, fear and isolation."

He laughed first, a good clean, happy guffaw she hadn't heard in a long time. Then he kissed her, hard, quick and deep. The drizzle turned back to rain, and they stood on the riverbank with their arms locked around each other until they were forced to come up for air.

Matt put his face to the shower. "You make me feel so damned human! It's been weeks."

"Since someone told you they believed in you?"

He turned and wiped rainwater off her chin. "That, too."

The walk back was devoted to Bridget because Matt insisted. He made her describe every detail of fundraising that she'd learned. When she'd finished with what had been accomplished for his hospital, she described the Christmas year-end packages going out. She talked about marketing, direct mail and working in Copley Square. It wasn't enough. He wanted to know about dairy farming.

They'd reached Marlborough Street. "I'm saving the dairy business until we eat. Otherwise we'll run out of conversation."

"Never."

She was beginning to think he was right and she was as buoyed by his newfound spirit as he was.

Matt went up to his own apartment long enough to discard his slicker and change into dry jeans and when he returned, Bridget had set out lunch. She'd transformed the chicken into a salad but included almonds, grapes, currants and bits of orange. There was a fresh green salad, as well, biscuits and white wine.

"Manna from heaven," Matt remarked.

"Old family recipe."

"I meant you."

"You look pretty good yourself, Doc."

"Do I, Bridget?"

"Yes," she replied. "You look content, maybe even relieved." He also looked very, very sexy, and as the old desire began its spiral, she motioned to the table. "You must be starving."

"For a lot of things."

"Chicken is what's on the menu, Matthew."

"Then by all means, let's start with the chicken."

They continued to talk as they ate and Bridget laughed at Matt's effort to slow down. "A real meal," he murmured. "Erin used to do this for Nancy and me when she could."

"There's something about good cooking."

"It's more than the food, Bridget. This is delicious and I love it."

"But?"

"No buts. I'm touched and I appreciate the effort you put into it. I appreciate the time you took to make it for me and set the table and have everything nice."

"You needed a decent meal."

"I needed the conversation just as much."

"You also needed to be forced into the rain for that walk."

"You make me feel whole." He stopped and sipped his wine. "Kevin said that to me about Erin just before the wedding ceremony."

"Did he?" She looked at her plate and poked a grape.

"Yes, and I'm beginning to understand what he meant. Bridget, hang around for a while, will you? Don't let anyone sweep you off your feet. Not yet."

She laughed. "Am I *that* vulnerable?"

"I don't know. I wish to hell I had the time to find out."

"Matt, I'm not going anywhere. I'm not even dating anybody at the moment."

"I don't have the right to ask you not to."

"Would you like to?"

He shook his head. "Not fair."

"That's not what I meant."

Matt finished his wine and reached over to caress her cheek. "Bridget I'd like to make love with you again, right here, upstairs, the supply closet—"

"Matt!"

"All right, but it's not fair to ask. I have nothing to give in return, least of all love."

"No, it wouldn't be love. You're in an emotional vice right now. That's self-preservation. You're still adjusting."

"I haven't even had a decent conversation for weeks. I'm sorry I talked so much this afternoon. I'm not the gut-spilling type."

"Don't ever be sorry! I could talk to you and listen forever. I want to help."

"Thank you, Bridget. You do."

"I've missed you, Matt." She got up from the table, plate in hand. "It'll probably be weeks till we can do this again, but I'd like to. It makes me feel as though I make a difference."

He put the rest of the dishes on the counter next to her. "You make an enormous difference." He shoved his hands in his pockets, closed his eyes and leaned back.

She watched him and smiled. "Matthew, are you trying not to kiss me?"

With his eyes still closed he muttered, "That obvious, huh?"

"Then I don't dare kiss you."

He opened his eyes. "You were considering it?"

"I couldn't help myself."

"Do you think it would help if I stood in ice water?"

"I'd need the ice water, as well."

He sighed happily. "I thought so. If we're both so damned hungry, then why can't we just eat!"

"Maybe I could, Matt. After all, I've seen Todd twice and I don't feel a thing. I almost went to Atlanta to escape and there's nothing to run from. I could see Todd anytime without even a twinge of desire."

"Will you?"

She shrugged. "I might. If he asks." Matt opened his mouth and she pressed her fingers against it. "No lectures. I'm over him and I'm not vulnerable, at least not the way you think I am." She leaned against him and felt the shock of it ripple through him. "However, there have been nights when I thought I'd go crazy with wanting *you*."

"Bridget, don't say that to somebody in my condition."

"Nothing's equal in this friendship at the moment. I'm not sure I could walk into that bedroom with you and be the same person tomorrow. I don't have an ICU to keep me distracted. I'm not so dead on my feet that wanting you doesn't flare up every once in a while."

"God."

"But I'd want the walks in the rain, too, and a whole lot more. It's been the cart before the horse since the day we met." As if to prove it, she stepped forward and put her arms around his neck. His embrace was a bear hug, wonderfully warm, erotic in its rush.

She was already breathing softly against his chest, giving herself the luxury of relaxing against him. She felt him strain against the rising passion in her, as if he could fight it long enough to propose a solution. But there wasn't a solution and they both knew it. There was only the moment and the desire coursing through them.

Once again they belonged to that rush and she knew she was incapable of remaining aloof from her own aching need. Tears welled up as her throat grew tight.

Matt chose that moment to kiss her, and the tears held while stronger emotions gripped her. He plundered her mouth and began the exploration she remembered so vividly. She loved him. It was all painfully clear. Gradually, as he sensed her turmoil, he stopped.

"Bridget?"

"We can't make love again. It isn't love and it isn't the supply closet. It's some nebulous area in between."

"We could make it work," he groaned.

"Darling Dr. Branigan, I'm not that strong."

Pain shot through his expression, draining the hope and pleasure so quickly it hurt to look. She leaned against his chest. "I want to say yes. I want to be there for you, Matt, to help make your life easier. But I can't. Not at the expense of my own emotions."

"Millbrook was a huge mistake. You were right."

"Maybe. What if we wound up like Erin and Kevin? What if all this fun leads to pregnancy? It was right for them but it would be disastrous for us. All three of us. More than anything else in the world, I want your friendship. I want to help and be there for you."

"But until I can do the same, there's nothing more to say."

"That's not the way I would have put it."

"Different words wouldn't make any difference. The hell of it is, you're right. You're not some ship in the night, Bridget, you never have been. You're the best friend I've got."

Her tears blurred her vision.

"Don't do that. I've been hung by my heels already this month. I can't handle tears, not from someone I care so much about."

"Then keep it to a handshake, Doc," she muttered.

He put out his hand and after shaking hers, ran it through her wild red hair.

Twelve

Bridget was tired of thinking how easy it would have been to have made love with Matt. She ran it around six ways to Sunday and it still came out the same: ecstasy for the moment, regret soon thereafter. Self-congratulations didn't do much to boost her spirits, and the fact that Matt seemed to be avoiding her didn't, either.

The first week he was apt to knock on his way up the stairs, if the hour was decent. She made him a freezer full of casseroles, for which he gave her a hug and bought her flowers. What she wanted was long, heartfelt conversation and the chance to listen and soothe his exhausted spirit.

Avoidance was difficult to diagnose in a man spending more hours at the hospital than at his apartment, but even after September closed and he'd finished with the intensive care unit rotation, he was still a rare sight.

Bridget had an invitation to Millbrook over the up-coming Columbus Day weekend. The harvest was in full swing and there were promises to put her to work if she arrived. Erin had made her promise that she would pressure Matt to get away, too.

Bridget taped a note on his door and at seven-thirty the following morning as he came home, he rapped on her door, looking like he'd slept in the alley, because, of course, he hadn't slept at all.

"Millbrook?" he asked, note in hand.

"It would do you some good. Even for the day. Are you off at all?"

"Sunday's swing day. I might be able to manage it."

Bridget touched his shoulder. "Make an effort, Matt, for your own mental health. Come down and be with people who love you. Healthy people. Erin's due any day and she wants you most of all."

"To calm Kevin down, no doubt."

"You don't need a reason. You need fresh air, manual labor and all those brothers. I'd like to see you, too. We need to catch up, even if we have to go to Millbrook to do it."

"It's been a while."

She wished there'd been more regret in his voice.

Bridget drove to Millbrook Friday after work and stayed up only long enough to get instructions for the next day's work. Erin was nearly bedridden and sleeping as much as possible, having been told she was ready to deliver but still four weeks from her due date.

Kevin, to combat his own work fatigue, was in bed by nine and it was the same for his brothers, as well.

Saturday morning after breakfast, Erin propped herself on cushions in the great room, wedged into the couch, in an effort to get comfortable. Nothing worked.

"Keep Kevin busy today," she told Bridget. "Go out and get fouled in your waders. Play helpless. Ask for advice. I don't care what else you do, but the man needs a diversion. I want him outside so I can lie here and feel lousy without his feeling guilt-ridden for procreating."

"Guilt-ridden for procreating!"

Erin grinned. "The night we created these little darlings, I tried to talk him out of it. At first, that is. Then it seemed like a good idea."

"It *does* take two."

"Takes two and we've made two. Now he's panicked that I'll slip into a childbirth coma or the babies'll arrive on the couch."

"Shades of Holly and Drew?"

"It was a blizzard then, not a harvest, I keep telling him. You'd think no one else on earth had ever given birth."

"As far as Kevin's concerned, no one else has."

"The man I really need is Matt. He's a doctor and he can knock some sense into his brother. Do you think he'll make it?"

"I know he'll try."

The sultry summer had been transformed into clear, warm days and cool nights. The last of the bogs at the homestead had been flooded. Jody and Ryan, atop the gangly "egg beaters," ran the paddle machinery through the crop, driving the plump, tart berries off their vines and up to the surface of the water. Yellow and orange sugar maples lined the acreage that Bridget never tired of looking at.

She put on a borrowed pair of waders and joined Megan in the bog, taking time to tease her sister about lending a hand with corralling the berries.

Both women looked out at Jody. "It must be love," Megan muttered.

Bridget looked her over. "You look very alluring in waders and Jody's old shirt."

"This is not what I had in mind for a holiday weekend."

"Will you ever get used to it?" Bridget asked.

Megan smiled. "I think I have already."

They were interrupted by the familiar sight as Matt Branigan's car pulled down the long driveway, and just the glimpse of the driver made Bridget grin.

He's here. It was an effort to stay where she was. From a distance he looked rested. She thought there was a spring in his step as he hailed his brothers and was hailed in return. Bridget counted on her fingers—it had been seven months since she'd first watched him walk that stretch of Branigan lawn. He was wearing the same green sweater, the one that matched his eyes.

"Get into some waders—no free ride this weekend," Sean called from the loading belt of the panel truck receiving the harvested berries.

"I'm making a house call," he yelled back. "I hear somebody's about to deliver twins."

"Erin knows enough to wait until the last bog's dry to go into labor." Sean threw back. "Cranberry growers aren't supposed to have children during the harvest."

"You might have mentioned that to Kevin last February," Matt shot back.

Bridget laughed with the rest of them. Matt was a different person already.

Matt came back outside half an hour later, dressed as the rest were in old clothes. He still looked tired but no more so than his brothers, who were losing sleep over monitoring bog temperatures and, in Drew's case, tending to new babies.

Bridget waved to him and waded through the shin-high water and joined him on the bank. "I'm glad you could make it."

"So am I."

"Everything's in good hands at the hospital?"

"Yes, indeed. I slept for once and rounds went well. All in all, I'm in decent shape." He leaned back against the truck. "Look at those maples. I never get tired of this."

Bridget worked side-by-side with him for another hour. He was quiet but the moodiness she worried about wasn't evident. The silence was comfortable and so was the idle conversation that family members kept to family matters.

At Matt's suggestion, Bridget stooped long enough to accompany him inside to check on Erin. She was dozing.

"Hey, guys," she murmured, trying to sit up. "I'm glad you came in. Kevin within earshot?"

"Not even close," Matt replied as he took her pulse.

"Good. I'm getting mighty crampy but it's too soon." She pressed her distended stomach and grimaced.

"That looked like a little more than cramps, Erin," Matt said.

"Did it?" She was panting.

Matt nodded. "Time them if it happens again."

"Help me up first so I can use the bathroom." She made her way slowly through the kitchen to the powder room only to emerge ashen. "I think you'd better call Kevin. I'm bleeding. Time to go, contractions or not."

Matt was next to her immediately. "Bright red, fresh?"

"Yes. Not much."

Matt ministered to his sister-in-law while Bridget calmly walked back out and found Kevin.

Leaving in the midst of six men, six women, three children and an infant was not to be uneventful. "This is your big chance to forget the hospital and let us deliver them here," Ryan quipped. "Sean and I can save you the trip."

"Thank you, no." Erin laughed and kissed her nieces, Kate, Suzanne and Maria, hugged Megan and then came to Bridget. "I can't wait," she said through shallow panting.

"Contraction?" Bridget whispered.

"Sort of."

"Good luck. I can't wait, either."

Matt waved his car keys as Kevin eased Erin into his Corvette but the eldest Branigan pushed them away. "It's your day off. Forget it."

"Call when you know anything," Matt answered.

"Drop her off and come back. You've left half a bog unfinished," Jody shouted.

"Clowns," Erin called as they left. "Every one of you."

Hours later, when the Branigans broke for the day, there was still no word. The brothers separated after reviewing the nights' assignments and gleaning promises from Bridget and Matt that they would call the minute they heard anything.

Soon a comfortable silence filled the autumn air in place of the hum of machinery and the day's conversation. Back inside the homestead, Bridget found Matt in the great room, eyes closed, on the couch. "I'm not asleep," he said as she tiptoed through.

"Then I'll make you some dinner."

Matt helped; they ate and waited. When there was no word from Kevin by nine, it was Bridget who called the shots. "I'm going to lock up. You go get some sleep. I'll read for a while."

"Would you?"

"Sure."

"Bridget?"

She looked up from the kitchen counter she was wiping.

"I enjoyed watching you work with my family. You fit here well. Better than I do."

"This is your home, Matt."

"It was." He sighed and started for the hallway.

She caught up with him at the stairs. "You can't leave me with that!"

"I'm one of them, but I'm not. It's always been that way. I've done something different, followed another path all my life."

"There are no two Branigans alike, Matthew, even I know that. They may all be on the bogs at the moment, but that doesn't make them alike. That doesn't make you excluded, either."

He sat down on the riser and she came next to him. "What is it, really? What set this off?"

"Damned if I know. Maybe Erin, maybe Kevin. Sean and Annie? Your guess is as good as mine. I'm too tired half the time to figure it out."

"Loss? The fact that you've gone beyond this? That you've really left home?"

He sank his head into his hands, then looked up at her. "Loss." He pressed his fist against his breastbone. "Want—an ache for something I don't have."

"What could that possibly be?"

"You said it the day we walked in the rain, and it's haunted me ever since. I live alone. There's nobody to bounce the depression off of. I'm lonely, Bridget, bone-aching lonely. I ache for what they all have."

"Love, Matthew. It's the only thing missing, and you'll have time for that, eventually."

"And until then? Until 'eventually' I'm supposed to muddle through. Be a good doctor, conscientious, forthright, hardworking to the detriment of every other aspect of my life. What the hell kind of physician will I make if that's all there is to my life?"

"A wonderful one. There's no doubt of that."

"Everyone's so damned sure but me."

"Then trust everyone. They know. I know," she finished softly.

His green eyes were dark when he looked at her again. "We were so close that rainy day, so close you backed away."

"I had to."

"I know that, but everything's been lousy since. I feel as though I touched what everybody else has, but I had to let go. I had to give it back. Do you understand that? I'm within reach, but I can't have it."

"Love?"

"Love. You. It's one in the same."

"You love me?"

"More so seeing you here. This is where we had time. Millbrook and this house are where we were two different people. Maybe that's the problem, seeing you here again. Knowing what we had."

"I miss those days."

"I loved them. I love you enough to keep away. Enough not to ask you to wait. Enough to be crazy with worry that you'll find somebody else and when I finally come out of this hole they call internship, you'll be gone."

She smiled at him. "You were right way back in April, if that's what you've been doing. You really don't know the first thing about love."

Matt sighed. "I have no right to ask you to wait."

"So you haven't asked."

"Of course not. Half the time I'm too busy to think about you, and the rest of the time I'm too obsessed with you to think about anything else. You're the closest thing I've got to a sounding board or a best friend.''

''That's a good place to start.''

''Loneliness is eating away at me. I want what the rest of the world has. The hell of it is that I've watched you get over Todd. I wanted you to, I hoped that you would. You recovered so entirely, it's as if your relationship with him never happened. I watched you put me at arm's length as if we never happened, either.''

She gathered her words before she spoke. ''I made it look easy?''

''God, yes.''

''You gave me the impression there was nothing to get over.''

''I had to.''

''Matt, I've had to convince myself that we didn't have anything but a little fun. Our making love didn't mean much to you so I couldn't let it mean much to me.''

''Didn't mean much!''

''Couldn't. 'No time for love, no time for commitments.' You drummed all of that into me.''

''I was drumming it into myself like so much circus hype. If it meant nothing to you, then I couldn't let it get to me.''

''And you're telling me it didn't work?''

''I'm telling you that I love you. I love you, Bridget, no matter how little time I've got, how many worries or responsibilities. You make all of it bearable.''

''Not having you has been unbearable,'' she whispered.

He caught her tremulous smile and traced it with his index finger. "Will you wait? I have no right to ask, but I have to know."

Slowly she shook her head. "I can't wait."

"Then I'm going back to Boston." He stood up but she yanked him back down beside her.

"Let me finish."

"I can't wait because I want you now. I want to make sense of your schedule and make sure you sleep. I want to get used to tiptoeing around and taking your calls. I want to make things work right now, Matt. At least we could try."

"It won't be romantic. It will be boring, trying. You'll have to live your own life, go places without me—"

"I know that."

"What I'm saying is that you'll have to settle for reality."

"I'll settle for you asleep next to me or gone for two days as long as I know that you love me."

"I have from the first. From the time I stood downstairs and watched you walk the dike, I felt it."

She pulled his hand to her breast where her heart hammered. "Feel it now."

He stood up and this time she followed. Without talking they went into her room and stood in the dark facing each other. Slowly, as if they'd made love just hours before, they undressed each other. There was no hurry—yet.

When their clothes were at their feet, Matt touched her breasts and moaned. "Next time we'll make it last, but now . . ." He filled his lungs. "Bridget, only twice in all these months...and you're all I've wanted.'' He circled the tender tips with his thumbs as she made wide sweeps over his chest.

''Hurry then. I can't wait, either.''

They began to rush, making similar, faster circles until their breathing was labored and desire danced from one to the other and back again.

She arched her back as the roughness of his skin heightened the sensation of his hands still on her breasts. She cried out his name and quickly he cupped the softness and played with the weight. His palms were warm.

She slid her hand down to his hips, along the length of him while he played and the more intimate she got, the deeper and faster the heat moved through her own body. Incredible heat began its ascent up through her chest and then down again.

''The spiral,'' she whispered. She let the sensation flow this time, no longer fighting it. ''Every time I've ever touched you...every time I'm with you, I'm filled with heat that shoots through me.''

''I know the feeling.'' He took her hand and brought it down to him. ''It starts here and runs up, through my heart, into my chest.'' He leaned forward and she held his head to her breasts. He began the kissing that she longed for, the trail of moisture at once hot, then cold in the October air, then hot again.

When her knees would no longer support her, she fell back onto the bed, bringing Matt with her. ''Next time,'' she panted.

''All night, I promise.''

"I can't believe you're here, that I'm really in your arms." The moment she'd finished, she kissed him, everywhere she could touch, and he did the same.

Matt's mouth forced the heat roaming through her to skim over her skin, as well. She was flushed with wanting him, heady with the knowledge that she was touching him again at last.

With the last bits of self-control she could maintain, she covered him with kisses. He was rock hard, tight with want. "You feel so good," he groaned, "I've dreamed of this." He was never still and the magic in his hands deepened everything she'd ever felt.

"Make it come true," she moaned as she reciprocated. They were racing their internal clocks, nearly desperate for release, oblivious to anything but the exquisite joy of finally being together.

She shifted as he hovered over her and cried out with him as he joined her. They rocked, one against the other, then together, then apart, each offering more to the other than they took for themselves.

That was the key, and suddenly, as Matt engulfed her in his arms, he shuddered. "I love you," she cried, and at that moment they soared.

Their embrace stayed tight through the long, sensual descent from ecstasy to an incredible dreamy place. "Stay with me," she whispered.

"Always." They fell asleep in each other's arms.

The phone rang just after midnight and Bridget answered it with one arm still around Matt.

"Bridget, it's Kevin. Did I wake you?"

"You promised you would. We've been waiting."

"I have some news, finally."

"Tell me everything."

"Erin's doing fine—she's dozing. I'm right in the room with her."

"And the babies? Are they both fine?"

There was an imperceptible pause. "The fetal monitor picked up a third heartbeat, just before six last night."

"Kevin!"

His voice broke. "It's been the longest night of my life. Erin was a trooper."

"Is she all right?"

"She's wonderful. We've got three sons, Bridget. Will you pass the news along?"

"Three?"

"They're beautiful. Perfect. Thirty fingers and thirty toes."

"Kevin!"

"I know. I'm just now absorbing it. They're fine, too. Premature and in the special nursery, but they say everything's fine. I'll catch some sleep here and be home in the morning."

"Sleep while you can!" She was about to hang up. "Names! Do they have names?"

"We gave the first two the names of our fathers— Hugh O'Connor Branigan, and James David Branigan III. We'll call him Jamie, my dad's nickname."

"And the third?"

"The third name Erin insisted on. Kevin Patrick III. That was my grandfather's name, too. We'll call him Kip."

"Hugh, Jamie and Kip. Oh, Kevin."

"As a physician Matt can come back to the nursery with me tomorrow. You all can visit soon. Will you let him know? I assume he's asleep so don't wake him."

Bridget looked at the peaceful expression on Matt's face as he lay next to her. "I won't. I'll call the others, and if Matt doesn't wake up, you can tell him yourself when you get home."

"I'd like to tell him. We've been through a lot—Matthew, Erin and I."

"I know. Kiss Erin for me. Kevin?"

"Yes?"

"Matt and I have some news, too. It can wait till we see you."

Epilogue

―――

Twenty-one months later

The Millbrook Ledger,
Millbrook, Massachusetts, June 25

AROUND TOWN

For friends and family of Millbrook's Branigan clan, Bittersweet Bogs was the place to be yesterday as Megan Smith O'Connor and Bridget Elizabeth O'Connor became the brides of James David Branigan, Jr. and Matthew Kennedy Branigan, M.D., respectively.

Under perfect skies, Hugh S. O'Connor of Valley View Farm, Dean's Corner, New Jersey, gave his daughters in marriage and then presided over the garden reception. The brides are also the daughters of the late Erin Flynn O'Connor. The grooms are the sons of the late James D. and Kathleen Ryan Branigan. The joint ceremony was performed by Monsignor Patrick Hackman of St. Mary's-on-the-Common, Millbrook, and the Reverend Michael Jacobs of Trinity Church, Dean's Corner.

To keep it all in the family, matron of honor and best man for the couples were sister of the brides Erin O'Connor Branigan and eldest brother of the grooms, Kevin P. Branigan, who were married in Millbrook two years ago.

Megan Branigan wore her mother-in-law's wedding gown of antique lace and Bridget Branigan wore her mother's, composed of satin and hemmed in seed pearls.

Young nieces and nephews of the couples served as attendants. Applause broke out as the older girls, each holding the hand of a toddler cousin, distributed flowers to the guests from baskets they carried. They were Suzanne G. Branigan, Kathleen R. Branigan, Maria B. Branigan, Peter A. Branigan and triplets, Hugh O'Connor, James D. III, and Kevin P. Branigan III. Ring bearer was Robert S. O'Connor, Jr. of Dean's Corner, second cousin of the brides.

Both couples are members of the Saquish Yacht Club in Plymouth and the Catboat Association as well as the Millbrook Country Club.

Megan O'Connor Branigan is a graduate of Blair Academy, Blairstown, New Jersey, and Cedar Crest College, Allentown, Pennsylvania. Former public service associate for Hackettstown, New Jersey, Radio Group, she is currently director of public service for Plymouth radio station WJQG.

James D. Branigan, Jr., is a graduate of Millbrook High School, Brown University and the Law School of Boston University. He served as environmental attorney for Hammell, Price and Bennett of Plymouth before opening his own law practice in Millbrook. He is also chief counsel for the Cranberry Growers Association of Southern Massachusetts and a partner in Branigan Cranberries, Inc. and Bittersweet Bogs, the family business in Millbrook.

Following a honeymoon on Nantucket, Mr. and Mrs. Kevin Branigan will reside in Millbrook.

Bridget O'Connor Branigan, of Boston, is a graduate of Dean's Corner High School and Barrett College for Women, Peterborough, New Hampshire. Dr. Branigan, also of Boston, is a graduate of Millbrook High School, Harvard University and Harvard Medical School.

Following a brief sailing honeymoon off Cape Cod, Dr. and Mrs. Branigan will return to Boston where she will continue as a fund-raising specialist for Back Bay Associates of Copley Square. Dr. Branigan, who served his internship at New England Regional Hospital, will continue his residency in pediatrics at Children's Hospital Medical Center.

*   *   *   *   *

SILHOUETTE® Desire™

COMING NEXT MONTH

#559 SUNSHINE—Jo Ann Algermissen
A Florida alligator farm? It was just what ad exec Rob Emery *didn't* need! But sharing the place with Angelica Franklin made life with the large lizards oh, so appealing....

#560 GUILTY SECRETS—Laura Leone
Leah McCargar sensed sexy houseguest Adam Jordan was not *all* he claimed. But before she could prove him guilty of lying, she became guilty... of love.

#561 THE HIDDEN PEARL—Celeste Hamilton
Aunt Eugenia's final match may be her toughest! Can Jonah Pendleton coax shy Maggie O'Grady into leading a life of adventure? The next book in the series *Aunt Eugenia's Treasures*.

#562 LADIES' MAN—Raye Morgan
Sensible Trish Becker knew that Mason Ames was nothing more than a good-looking womanizer! But she still couldn't stop herself from succumbing to his seductive charms.

#563 KING OF THE MOUNTAIN—Joyce Thies
Years ago Gloria Hubbard had learned that rough, tough William McCann was one untamable man. Now he was back in town... and back in her life.

#564 SCANDAL'S CHILD—Ann Major
When May's *Man of the Month* Officer Garret Cagan once again saved scandalous Noelle Martin from trouble, the Louisiana bayou wasn't the only thing steaming them up....

AVAILABLE NOW:

#553 HEAT WAVE
Jennifer Greene

#554 PRIVATE PRACTICE
Leslie Davis Guccione

#555 MATCHMAKER, MATCHMAKER
Donna Carlisle

#556 MONTANA MAN
Jessica Barkley

#557 THE PASSIONATE ACCOUNTANT
Sally Goldenbaum

#558 RULE BREAKER
Barbara Boswell

AVAILABLE NOW—

the books you've been waiting for by one of America's top romance authors!

DIANA PALMER

DUETS

Ten years ago Diana Palmer published her very first romances. Powerful and dramatic, these gripping tales of love are everything you have come to expect from Diana Palmer.

This month some of these titles are available again in **DIANA PALMER DUETS**—a special three-book collection. Each book has two wonderful stories plus an introduction by the author. You won't want to miss them!

Available now at your favorite retail outlet.

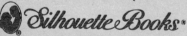 *Silhouette Books* ®

DP-1A

Silhouette Special Edition

proudly presents

Taming Natasha
by
NORA ROBERTS

Once again, award-winning author Nora Roberts weaves her special brand of magic this month in TAMING NATASHA (SSE #583). Toy shop owner Natasha Stanislaski is a pussycat with Spence Kimball's little girl, but to Spence himself she's as ornery as a caged tiger. Will some cautious loving sheath her claws and free her heart from captivity?

TAMING NATASHA, by Nora Roberts, has been selected to receive a special laurel—the Award of Excellence. This month look for the distinctive emblem on the cover. It lets you know there's something truly special inside.

Available now